"You have to come see this," C. T. told Lea.

Reluctantly, Lea got up from her chair and shuffled over to where C. T. was kneeling on the floor.

"Look." He pointed to the label on the box. It said, "Grandpa's Monster Movies."

"Cool!" Lea said. "Now this could be fun."

C. T. was already digging into the box. The movies inside were on old-fashioned reels, just like the home movies. But the titles on the reels were things like Frankenstein, and Dracula, and The Wolfman.

"I didn't know Grandpa was into old horror movies," Lea said.

As C. T. went through the titles trying to decide which one to watch, he found something in the box that nearly stopped his heart cold. . . .

DEADTIME STORIES™

Grandpa's Monster Movies

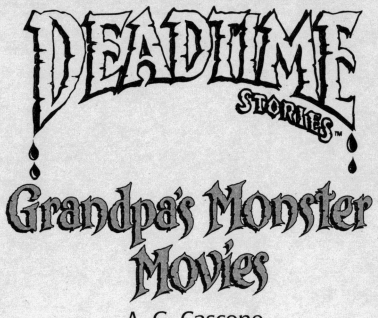

DEADTIME STORIES™

Grandpa's Monster Movies

A. G. Cascone

Troll

For Roy—
for taking such good care
of his two little monster-authors
and
For Lea and Rose—
for having such a great dad.

CHAPTER 1

Catan Thomas was lost—hopelessly lost.

Worse than that, he was being hunted.

He thought he was well hidden. But then, so were his hunters.

They might be anywhere, Catan Thomas thought. *They might be just a few feet away right now!*

There was no way for him to know. He couldn't see more than a foot in any direction, because he was deep inside a cornfield, surrounded by stalks that towered high above his head.

It had seemed like the perfect place to hide. But now he wasn't so sure. Now he felt swallowed up by the field.

The cornstalks stood so close together that Catan Thomas could barely move between them. Still, he kept going, hoping that eventually he would make it to safety.

He tried to be quiet. But he couldn't avoid rustling the leaves of the plants as he passed by them.

He was aware of every sound he made. In a way, that made him feel safe. He figured that if *he* couldn't move through the cornfield without making noise, neither could anyone else. No one would be able to catch him off guard.

Unless they were sitting quietly, waiting!

That thought stopped Catan Thomas dead in his tracks.

Now what? he thought.

Before he could decide, he heard a sudden rustle and was grabbed from behind.

"Aaaggghhh!" he screamed.

A hand closed over his mouth.

"Shut up," a voice commanded.

He did as he was told.

"It's just me, C. T.," the voice whispered in his ear.

It took him a moment to realize that the voice belonged to his cousin, Lea Rose.

"They almost got me," she told him as she removed her hand from his mouth.

"How did you get away?" he asked.

"I ran!" she said as if he were stupid. "I don't know if they followed me, but I don't think we should stay here. We've got to keep moving."

"Yeah," C. T. agreed. "But which way?"

Lea Rose shrugged hopelessly.

"This is a nightmare," C. T. said. "We're being stalked in a cornfield."

"By a bunch of hillbillies," Lea Rose added.

"The worst part is that we're actually related to those hillbillies." C. T. groaned.

"They're *distant* cousins," Lea Rose reminded him.

"Not distant enough," C. T. complained. "I wish I'd never met these people. I'm never coming to another family reunion as long as I live."

"I know what you mean," Lea Rose agreed. "I can't believe we have to spend another two whole days here in Bumbleweed. I don't know how Grandma and Grandpa can stand to live out here in the middle of nowhere." Lea Rose shook her head in disbelief.

"Yeah," C. T. nodded. "But don't forget, your mom and my dad grew up on this farm too."

Lea's mom and C. T.'s dad were Grandma and Grandpa's children. They were the *normal* side of the family. The problem was that Grandpa had two brothers—Ernie and Earl—who weren't very normal at all.

Ernie was the youngest brother. He'd been struck by lightning—sixteen different times. It was amazing that Ernie had even survived. But aside from lightning bolt number two, which left Uncle Ernie with a "hair condition," and lightning bolt number nine, which gave him a "kick," Uncle Ernie claimed to be fine. Still, the rest of the family was quite clear on the fact that Uncle Ernie had sixteen holes in his head.

But Uncle Ernie wasn't nearly as big a problem as Earl, Grandpa's middle brother, because Uncle Ernie wasn't married. He lived with Grandma and Grandpa in their gigantic, old farmhouse. And *he* didn't have any kids.

Uncle Earl, the "raving maniac," *was* married. He and his wife, Luleen, had lots of kids, and lots of grandchildren—C. T.'s and Lea's *distant* cousins. Cousins that C. T. and Lea were forced to be nice to.

That was the real problem. Because the cousins were a *real* scary bunch.

"We don't have time to stand around talking," Lea said. "We've got to find our way back to the house before those weirdos catch up to us."

She shoved C. T. to get him moving.

But C. T. stood frozen right where he was.

"Listen," he whispered to Lea.

They heard the rustle of cornstalks.

Someone was headed toward them, but C. T. couldn't figure out from which direction. They had to know that before they started running. C. T. wanted to make sure they were running *away* from the drooling stalkers and not toward them.

Lea pointed to the right.

C. T. listened for another moment, then decided she was right. He grabbed her hand and started running to the left.

But as they ran, whoever was chasing them began moving more quickly.

C. T. heard the stalks crack and pulled Lea along even faster. But he knew they weren't going to get away this time.

Their pursuer was gaining on them with lightning speed.

C. T. looked back over his shoulder.

Less than ten feet behind them, he saw the cornstalks part as they broke and fell.

But nobody was there.

It was as if an invisible force was causing the damage.

"What's going on?" C. T. cried as he kept running.

The cornstalks behind them continued to snap and fall. Whatever was chasing them was about to overtake them.

It was only three feet away when C. T. finally saw what was after them.

It was like nothing he'd ever seen in his life. And it definitely wasn't one of his cousins.

CHAPTER 2

"What is that thing?" Lea shrieked as the creature came within inches of them.

Something the size of a beach ball was rolling across the ground like a tumbleweed. It was brown and furry—and alive!

C. T. had no idea what it was. But one thing was certain—it didn't sound friendly. In fact, it was growling like a vicious dog as it rolled to a stop at their feet.

C. T. couldn't see the thing's face, but he had no doubt that it had teeth.

He was about to grab Lea's arm and run when the creature quickly rolled away from them.

Both C. T. and Lea watched, dumbfounded, as the giant fur ball snapped its way through the cornstalks until it was nothing more than a faint noise in the distance.

"What the heck *was* that thing?" Lea repeated the question.

"Beats me," C. T. answered.

"Do you think it was some kind of possum or something?" Lea asked.

"I doubt it," C. T. answered. He'd seen possums before, and he was pretty sure they didn't roll.

"So what do you think it was?" Lea wanted to know.

C. T. just shrugged. But curiosity was getting the better of him. "You want to try to follow it?" he asked Lea. "Maybe if we got another look at it, we could figure out what it is."

"Are you nuts?" Lea shot back. "That thing was growling!"

"Yeah, but it didn't attack us or anything," C. T. pointed out, "so how dangerous could it be?"

"Who knows?" Lea said.

"Oh, come on," C. T. urged. "Let's check it out."

"Fine," Lea finally gave in. "But if that thing bites me, you're dead."

C. T. began moving in the direction the fur ball had gone, with Lea right on his heels.

Whatever the fur ball was, it rolled pretty fast. The sound of rustling cornstalks ahead had faded quickly.

Still, C. T. kept moving forward, hoping that sooner or later he would catch up with the mysterious creature.

He ran faster and faster, pulling Lea along behind him.

Suddenly something blocked their path. Something far *worse* than a growling fur ball.

April and May, their twin cousins from Uncle Earl's side of the family, stood there. They were wearing matching gingham dresses with matching ruffled aprons, and their matching pigtails were tied with matching pink bows. They stared at C. T. and Lea with matching blank expressions.

April and May didn't say a word. They never did—except to one another, and then they whispered so that no one else could hear.

April and May were probably the creepiest of all the creepy cousins.

They were named April and May because one had been born just before midnight on the last day of April, while the other had been born right after midnight, on the first day of May. Nobody could tell which was which. Nobody seemed to care.

But one thing was certain—C. T. didn't want to have anything to do with either of them. He spun on his heel, making a one-hundred-eighty-degree turn, and pushed Lea in the opposite direction.

Equally anxious to get away from April and May, Lea was off and running even as C. T. pushed her.

But she had taken only a couple of steps before she stopped short, making C. T. bump into her.

"Move," he said, pushing her again.

She held her ground.

C. T. saw why.

They were surrounded. There was no place to run.

"It's over," one of their drooling captors informed them.

"We've got you now," a second chimed in.

"We've been caught by the Bobs," Lea groaned, putting her face in her hands.

The Bobs were the rest of the cousins from Uncle Earl's side of the family—Billy-Bob, Joe-Bob, Jimmy-Bob, and Bobby-Bob. April and May were known as the "Bobs' Twins." They were all about C. T.'s and Lea's age. That was why the grown-ups decided they should all play together.

The only game that C. T. and Lea would agree to play with the Bobs and the Bobs' Twins was hide-and-seek. But now that they'd been caught, it was the Bobs' turn to choose a game.

C. T. wasn't about to let that happen. And he had a perfect way to stop it.

"Did any of you guys see a weird, growling, fur ball rolling through the cornfield?" he asked.

They just stood there as if they were in a trance, except for Bobby-Bob.

His eyes widened and he began nodding his head enthusiastically. His lips began to move, but it took a while for words to actually start coming out. C. T. was convinced that Bobby-Bob's brain worked on a seven-second delay.

"I think I seen it," Bobby-Bob said as his head continued to nod.

You mean you saw it. C. T. wanted to correct Bobby-Bob's English, but it wasn't worth the trouble. So he stayed silent as Bobby-Bob went on.

"It was a strange little critter," Bobby-Bob told his brothers.

The rest of the Bobs looked at Bobby-Bob with the same disbelief they'd shown C. T.

"You probably just seen a tumbleweed," Billy-Bob laughed.

Saw! C. T.'s brain hollered. But he kept his mouth shut.

"It weren't no tumbleweed," Bobby-Bob insisted. "This critter was alive. I know that for a fact because I watched him catch a field mouse and eat it! Then the darnedest thing happened right before my very eyes. The furry little bugger grew till he was almost twice as big as he was before!"

"Get out of here," Joe-Bob said, shaking his head. "That's impossible. You're making this up."

"Am not," Bobby-Bob insisted.

"We saw it too," C. T. said.

Lea nodded her agreement. "It went that way." She pointed past April and May.

"Why don't we see if we can find it?" Jimmy-Bob suggested.

"We ought to head in different directions," C. T. added.

"Good thinking," Billy-Bob said. He was the leader of the Bobs, so the rest of them agreed.

C. T. couldn't believe it was going to be that easy to get rid of the Bobs and the Bobs' Twins.

But it was.

C. T. listened patiently as Billy-Bob sent each one of them in a different direction.

The Bobs were off in a flash, leaving C. T. and Lea alone with the Bobs' Twins. Though Billy-Bob had told the twins which way to go to look for the mysterious creature, neither one of them made a move to obey.

"Let's just head back toward the house," Lea whispered to C. T.

C. T. thought that was a pretty good idea—but he didn't know exactly where the house was. Since the most important thing was to stay as far away from the cousins as they could get, C. T. began leading Lea in the one direction that none of them had taken.

On and on they walked, hoping that sooner or later they would find their way out of the cornfield.

Suddenly something *big* blocked their path. And it was drooling a lot more than the Bobs.

CHAPTER 3

The creature that loomed over C. T. and Lea was nearly as big as King Kong—and almost as hairy.

But it wasn't Kong. It was Uncle Ernie, who *looked* just like Kong, thanks to lightning bolt number two.

Every inch of Uncle Ernie's skin was carpeted with wiry, black hair. It was so thick that if Uncle Ernie didn't have a head, there'd be no way to tell which direction he was facing. The hair on his back was as thick as the hair on his chest. Unfortunately, both of them always stuck out, because Uncle Ernie liked to wear his *over*alls without his *under*shirt.

Luckily, Uncle Ernie *did* have a head—and a spiffy clean shave, so C. T. could see his face clearly. And he could see that Uncle Ernie looked pretty upset.

So did his pet pig, Porkchop, who was standing beside

20

Uncle Ernie, pawing the ground and squealing up a storm.

"Everybody get out of the cornfield right now!" Uncle Ernie bellowed, waving his arms like a hairy windmill.

"What's wrong, Uncle Ernie?" Lea asked.

"Nothing," Uncle Ernie answered nervously. "Nothing at all."

Just then, Uncle Ernie's left eye started to twitch. C. T. knew that Uncle Ernie was lying. The "lying twitch" was a little glitch left by lightning bolt number three. It was supposed to be a secret, but everyone knew.

Something was wrong. Both Uncle Ernie and Porkchop knew what it was, but neither of them was willing to confess.

"It's time for supper," Uncle Ernie told C. T. and Lea. "Yeah. That's right," he said, more to himself than to them. "It's supper time. That's why everybody has to get out of the field—to eat supper."

"Hey, Uncle Ernie," Lea piped up. "We just saw the strangest thing."

Uncle Ernie's eyes widened with worry. So did Porkchop's. But neither one of them made a sound.

"It was a giant, growling fur ball," Lea went on. "It was rolling through the cornfield. Bobby-Bob saw it too."

"It must have been your imagination," Uncle Ernie said, shaking his head furiously. "There's no such thing around here. No such thing at all. I don't know what you're talking about."

But C. T. had the sneaking suspicion that Uncle Ernie knew exactly what they had seen. His left eye was twitching out of control.

"Now, get out of the cornfield," Uncle Ernie insisted. "Head toward the house where it's safe. I've got to go round up the Bobs and the Bobs' Twins before they go missing for good."

C. T. wouldn't have minded one bit if the Bobs and the Bobs' Twins "went missing for good." The problem was that C. T. had the distinct impression that they were *all* in danger.

"What's going on, Uncle Ernie?" C. T. asked.

Uncle Ernie didn't answer. But Porkchop pawed the ground furiously and squealed even more loudly than before.

"It's okay," Uncle Ernie assured Porkchop, patting his head. "Just stay calm. I'm going to get everything under control."

"What's out of control?" C. T. asked.

"Just you kids," Uncle Ernie answered. "Now hurry up and get over to the house like I told you." He pointed them in the right direction and gave them a little nudge to send them on their way.

C. T. watched over his shoulder as Uncle Ernie walked deeper into the cornfield calling for the Bobs and the Bobs' Twins, with Porkchop right at his heels.

C. T. and Lea walked less than ten feet before they emerged from the cornfield onto the lawn. They began running toward the house. C. T. couldn't wait to tell his parents what they'd seen in the cornfield and how strangely Uncle Ernie had acted about it.

But he never got the chance.

Because when they reached the house, they were confronted with a sight so horrible, all other thoughts disappeared from their minds.

CHAPTER

4

There were picnic tables set up on the back lawn. The grown-ups had decided that there were too many people to fit comfortably inside the dining room. Since it was nice weather, they decided it would be fun to eat outside.

But C. T. saw immediately that this wasn't going to be fun at all. On one table was some of the most putrid stuff that C. T. had ever seen in his life.

"What is that?" he asked Lea, grimacing in disgust.

"Beats me," Lea answered, sounding equally repulsed. "But it sure looks horrible."

"No, it ain't," another voice informed them. It was Aunt Luleen, Uncle Earl's wife. Somehow, she'd managed to sneak up on them. For a woman Aunt Luleen's size, that was a real trick. "You're lookin' at some real good eats there," she assured them. "I've spent days cookin' up a mess of my family's favorite vittles."

"Mess is certainly the word for it," Lea whispered to C. T.

Aunt Luleen didn't hear. She was too busy pointing out her special dishes. "That there's pickled pig's feet. That's pig's feet Parmesan. Then there's pig's feet and possum tail, knuckles and noodles, carameled coon, and ferret fricassee." After she'd finished, she reached for a pickled pig's foot and started to chow down.

"No wonder Porkchop's so jittery," C. T. whispered to Lea. "It looks like Aunt Luleen cooked up most of his relatives."

Lea's mom came up beside them.

"I'm not eating any of this slop," Lea told her. "I'll die."

C. T. nodded in agreement.

"Don't start," Lea's mom warned. "You two just smile and thank Aunt Luleen for working so hard."

"But, Mom . . ." Lea started to protest.

"But, Mom, nothing. In case you've forgotten, we're all here to celebrate Grandpa's seventieth birthday tomorrow. It's the first time this whole family has been together. And everybody's going to be nice."

"Leave the kids alone," Grandma said as she approached the table with a big plate of her famous fried chicken. Then she whispered to C. T. and Lea, "I don't blame you for not wanting to eat Luleen's cooking. I wouldn't. That's why I made some normal food." Then Grandma winked at them.

Aunt Luleen had long since stopped paying attention to C. T. and Lea. She had a new problem on her hands.

She was busy hollering at her son, Billy-Bob Senior. "You'd better stop eatin' up all that ferret fricassee before your daddy even gets himself a bite." She smacked Billy-Bob Senior's hand as he tried to take another spoonful. "Where is my honey-pie Earl anyway?" she asked Grandma.

"I think he's down by the barn with Eddie," Grandma answered. Eddie was C. T. and Lea's grandpa. "Why don't you two run down there and tell them supper's ready," Grandma said to C. T. and Lea, "before Luleen has herself a full-blown tizzy fit."

C. T. and Lea were more than happy to go. They'd do anything to get away from Earl's clan.

"They're over by the new barn," Grandma called after them. "Remember to stay away from the old barn. That thing's falling down and it's dangerous."

That was the millionth time they'd been reminded about that. Nobody was allowed to go near the old barn. C. T. didn't understand why Grandpa didn't just tear it down. But as he and Lea dashed past it, C. T. noticed that it really wasn't in such bad shape. He just shrugged and continued on to the new barn.

But as they approached the barn, C. T. heard angry voices coming from around the side.

He stopped Lea to listen.

"Stop acting like a raving maniac, Earl," C. T. heard Grandpa holler. C. T. was surprised to hear his grandfather sound so angry. C. T. had never before heard his grandfather raise his voice.

"I'm not acting like a raving maniac," Earl shouted back. "I'm dead serious. I've had enough of Ernie and all the problems he's caused. Before the end of this family reunion, I'm gonna chop that hairy critter to bits. And that's a promise."

C. T. peeked around the side of the barn to see what was going on.

What he saw made him jump back.

Uncle Earl obviously meant what he was saying. Because as he and Grandpa were arguing, Uncle Earl was busy sharpening the biggest axe that C. T. had ever seen.

CHAPTER 5

"There's not going to be any trouble at this family reunion," Grandpa warned Uncle Earl. "Do you hear me?"

Uncle Earl didn't answer.

"What are they talking about?" Lea whispered to C. T.

"Sounds like murder at the family reunion," C. T. whispered back. He got up the courage to peek around the corner again.

There was no doubt about it. Uncle Earl was definitely planning to do something bad. In addition to the axe he was sharpening, he had a pile of other scary-looking tools as well. There were buzz saws and pitchforks, a pickaxe, and a giant box marked "TNT."

"This is my birthday," Grandpa went on. "All the family is here together. This is going to be a happy time."

Earl laughed. It wasn't a nice laugh. It was a mean one.

"Yeah," he said. "Just like Floyd Garvey's birthday was happy."

"Let it go, Earl," Grandpa warned. "That was sixty years ago."

Earl didn't let it go. "That's right," he said. "Floyd Garvey's been gone for sixty years now—all because of Ernie."

"It wasn't Ernie's fault," Grandpa said. "It was Gus-Gus. We can't hold Ernie responsible for that."

"Ernie *is* responsible," Earl insisted. "And how many others have disappeared since then? Not to mention all the killings in the barn."

Killings in the barn? C. T. and Lea looked at one another in horror. What was going on out here in Bumbleweed?

"I'm going to take care of this situation once and for all," Earl said. "And there's nothing you can do to stop me."

"Let's get out of here," Lea whispered to C. T.

C. T. nodded his agreement. But as he turned to run, he tripped over a shovel that was leaning up against the side of the barn. Both he and the shovel fell over with a loud thud.

"Who's there?" Uncle Earl growled.

C. T. tried to scramble to his feet. But he tripped again, making even more noise.

"Is that you, Ernie?" Uncle Earl's voice got closer. "You Floyd-Garvey-murdering half-wit!"

Lea grabbed C. T.'s hand and dragged him to his feet.

But before they had a chance to run, Uncle Earl stalked around the side of the barn.

Both kids screamed as Uncle Earl stood over them, his newly sharpened axe raised over his head, ready to strike.

CHAPTER 6

C. T. was sure that he and Lea were done for.

"Earl!" Grandpa shouted, coming up behind him. "What do you think you're doing, scaring those children like that? Are you crazy?"

C. T. knew that the answer was yes.

In an instant, Grandpa had grabbed the axe from Uncle Earl's hands. "Don't pay any attention to Uncle Earl," Grandpa said, trying to sound calm. "He's just a cantankerous old coot."

"How long have you two been sneaking around this barn, listening to conversations that are none of your business?" Uncle Earl asked menacingly.

"We haven't been sneaking around the barn," C. T. stammered.

"We just got here," Lea added quickly.

"What did you hear?" Uncle Earl obviously didn't believe them.

"Nothing," C. T. lied.

"Grandma sent us down to tell you it's time to eat," Lea said.

"That's right!" C. T. agreed. It was the truth, after all. "Aunt Luleen wants you to hurry up before all the ferret fricassee is gone."

"And it's going fast," Lea added.

Grandpa had to put his hand over his mouth to stop from laughing.

But ferret fricassee was no laughing matter to Uncle Earl. "I'd better go get me some before Billy-Bob Senior sucks it all up," he said as he took off running for the house.

That left C. T. and Lea alone with Grandpa beside the barn.

For an uncomfortable moment, no one spoke. Then Grandpa said, "Why don't the two of you head on back to the house too. I'll be right behind you."

Obediently, C. T. started to walk away. Then he stopped. "Grandpa, what's Uncle Earl so upset about?" he asked.

Grandpa thought about it for a second. "Nothing for you to worry about," he said, shaking his head.

But C. T. could see that it was something that worried Grandpa, even though he was trying to smile reassuringly.

"But Grandpa . . ." Lea began to protest.

"Everything's fine," Grandpa insisted. "Now you'd better hurry along if you want to get some of Aunt Luleen's delicious ferret fricassee," he teased.

They all laughed at that one.

But nobody moved.

"Go on," Grandpa said finally.

C. T. and Lea turned away and started back toward the house.

But C. T. looked back over his shoulder to see Grandpa covering up Uncle Earl's stack of tools with a tarp. He saw Grandpa shake his head sadly.

"There's gonna be trouble around here again," Grandpa said to himself. "Big, big trouble!"

CHAPTER 7

"What's going on around here?" Lea asked C. T. as they headed back toward the house.

C. T. shrugged. He hadn't a clue. But one thing was certain. "Whatever it is, it's not good," he told her.

"I wish we could go home right now," she said. "Back to the safety of the city."

So did C. T. , especially when he saw the scene that awaited them.

All of Uncle Earl's side of the family, including the Bobs and the Bobs' Twins, were chowing down on Aunt Luleen's vittles as if there were no tomorrow.

C. T. totally lost his appetite. There was no way he could even eat any of Grandma's famous fried chicken while he watched Uncle Earl's clan sucking away on pig's feet and possum tails.

C. T. wasn't the only one who didn't like it.

Uncle Ernie's pet pig, Porkchop, was cowering under a tree, whimpering.

C. T. saw Aunt Luleen staring at Porkchop and drooling. So did Uncle Ernie. "Don't even think about it, Luleen," he said. "You leave my Porkchop alone. He's not an eatin' pig."

Aunt Luleen just laughed. "Every pig is an eatin' pig," she insisted. "Even a runt like that one."

"Just remember what they say, Luleen," Uncle Ernie shot back. "You are what you eat!"

Aunt Luleen ignored the insult. "I still remember his great-great-great-granddaddy, Hamhock! Now that was one delicious porker. Wasn't he, Earl?"

"Sure was," Uncle Earl agreed through a mouthful of ferret fricassee. "That bad boy won first prize at the county fair before we ate him."

C. T. and Lea pushed their plates away.

"Now those were the good old days," Aunt Luleen said.

C. T. could see that his mom and dad, and Lea's mom and dad, were trying real hard to smile and be polite through this disgusting conversation. But even they were only picking at the food that Grandma had prepared.

Grandpa finally joined the group, sitting next to Grandma and filling his plate with all the things that she had cooked. He smiled at Grandma. But the smile quickly faded. C. T. could tell that he was still deeply troubled by something.

But Aunt Luleen didn't seem to notice anybody else's

mood. She just went right on talking about "the good old days."

"We were just kids then, weren't we, honey-pie?" she said, patting Uncle Earl's hand.

Uncle Earl nodded as he let out a rip-roaring burp.

"Me and Earl's been in love since kindergarten," she announced to the rest of the group. "We had our first kiss at that county fair where Hamhock won the blue ribbon."

Everybody—even the Bobs and the Bobs' Twins—cringed at that information.

Grandma got up from the table and began uncovering the desserts that had been set out on another picnic table. C. T. and Lea followed her to help. Actually, they just wanted to get away from Aunt Luleen's conversation.

Besides, C. T. had a question he wanted to ask his grandmother.

"Grandma," he said when they were out of earshot of the rest of the family. "Who's Gus-Gus?"

"Gus-Gus?" Grandma repeated.

"Yeah," Lea said. "We heard Uncle Earl talking about him to Grandpa. Is he a member of the family?"

C. T. had a worse thought. "Is he coming to Grandpa's birthday party tomorrow?"

Grandma furrowed her brow and put her hands on her hips while she thought for a moment. "Gus-Gus," she said to herself. "No," she said finally. "I don't believe I ever met anybody named Gus-Gus. He must be somebody from a long time ago, before I met your grandpa."

C. T. hoped it was somebody who was long gone.

Because whoever Gus-Gus was, he sounded like nothing but trouble.

"I've got to go in the house and get the whipped cream for the pie," Grandma said as she headed away from the table.

C. T. and Lea stayed put. They didn't want to rejoin the others.

"Well, at least we won't have to worry about having to meet Gus-Gus—whoever he is," C. T. said to Lea.

Suddenly, someone grabbed the back of C. T.'s shirt and spun him around.

It was Uncle Earl, and he had a mean scowl on his face.

"Why are you talking about Gus-Gus, boy?" he demanded in a low voice.

C. T. began to stutter and stammer. "No reason," he answered finally.

Uncle Earl moved his face closer to C. T.'s until they were nose to nose. "Let me give you a word of advice," Uncle Earl whispered, his breath smelling of foul ferret fricassee. "If you know what's good for you, you'll forget that you ever heard that name!"

CHAPTER
8

"We've got to get away from all these weirdos," C. T. said to Lea after Uncle Earl stomped away. "I can't take it anymore."

"There's no place to go," Lea reminded him. "We're stuck with them. And our moms have told us ten thousand times how we have to be nice and play with our cousins."

C. T. looked over at the Bobs and the Bobs' Twins and shook his head hopelessly. "They're booger-eating morons," he groaned. "Look at what they're doing now."

The Bobs and the Bobs' Twins were all gathered around Grandpa's big brick barbecue. They were busy putting marshmallows on sticks so that they could poke them into the coals until the marshmallows caught fire. They let the marshmallows get nice and black before they blew out the fire and ate them.

"We can't 'play nice' with them," Lea groaned. "And we can't go on playing hide-and-seek for the next two days either."

"Hey," Billy-Bob said to the group around the barbecue. "After we're through with the marshmallows, what do you say we play a game of red-rover?"

"No way!" Lea said to C. T. "I'm not holding hands with any of them."

"Then we'd better beat it out of here fast," C. T. said.

"And go where?" Lea asked.

"Inside," C. T. said, heading toward the house.

The adults were going in and out of the house too, cleaning up after supper. C. T. and Lea dodged between them, moving through the kitchen and into the living room. But C. T. didn't stop there. He wasn't about to risk being sent back outside. He led Lea through the front hallway and upstairs.

There were more than half a dozen bedrooms on the second floor of the big old farmhouse.

"Which room do you want to hide in?" Lea asked C. T.

Before he could answer, another voice called out. "Catan Thomas! Lea Rose!" It was one of the Bobs.

C. T. put his finger up to his lips to tell Lea to be quiet. Footsteps started up the stairs.

Lea shrugged at C. T., silently asking, *What do we do now?*

C. T. looked around frantically, trying to decide. Then he spotted a door at the end of the hallway—a door that led up to the attic. He motioned for Lea to follow him and began tiptoeing quickly toward their only chance for escape.

"Catan Thomas? Lea Rose?" The voice got closer. "Are you up here? Want to play red-rover with us?"

C. T. shook his head no as he reached the door to the attic. He and Lea managed to slip through it just in time.

"Catan Thomas? Lea Rose?" The Bob wasn't giving up.

C. T. heard him moving down the hallway, calling into each room.

C. T. crept up the attic stairs, with Lea right behind him. Luckily, the Bob didn't follow.

"I think we're safe," C. T. said as they reached the top of the attic stairs.

"Yeah," Lea agreed. "But what are we going to do up here?"

C. T. looked around the dark, dusty attic. It was full of musty-smelling boxes and lots of old junk. It was obvious that Grandma and Grandpa didn't come up here very often.

C. T. looked around for a light switch, but he couldn't find one. He pulled the chain on the one bulb that was dangling from the ceiling. The only other light in the attic came from a small window at the far end. C. T. walked over to it and looked outside. The window faced the old barn.

"I don't want to stay up here," Lea complained.

"Our only other choice is to go downstairs and play red-rover with the Bobs," C. T. pointed out.

"Forget it," Lea said, plunking herself down in a dusty old chair. "I guess we'll just have to stay up here till we rot."

C. T. wasn't about to just sit there being bored. He started looking through the old boxes.

Most of them were filled with old clothes, books, and papers. But then C. T. came upon a box that looked interesting.

"Check it out," he said to Lea, who was still sitting in her chair, watching him. He reached into the box and pulled out a movie reel. "This whole box is full of home movies."

Lea just laughed at C. T. as she shook her head. "We can't stand being in Bumbleweed," she pointed out. "Why on earth would we want to watch old home movies from here?"

"Oh, come on," C. T. urged. "It's not like we have anything better to do." He grabbed for the old movie projector that was sitting behind the box of movies. Behind that, he saw a screen. And behind that was yet another box. This one was sure to arouse Lea's attention.

"You have to come see this," he told her.

Reluctantly, Lea got up from her chair and shuffled over to where C. T. was kneeling on the floor.

"Look." He pointed to the label on the box. It said, "Grandpa's Monster Movies."

"Cool!" Lea said. "Now this could be fun."

C. T. was already digging into the box. The movies inside were on old-fashioned reels, just like the home movies. But the titles on the reels were things like Frankenstein, Dracula, and The Wolfman.

"I didn't know Grandpa was into old horror movies," Lea said.

As C. T. went through the titles trying to decide which one to watch, he found something in the box that nearly stopped his heart cold.

CHAPTER 9

"What is it?" Lea asked as C. T. stared into the box with his mouth agape.

He reached inside the box, grabbed the reel that had caught his attention, and handed it to her.

When she saw the title, she gasped. "Gus-Gus," she read out loud.

"Gus-Gus," C. T. repeated, remembering the conversation they'd overheard between Grandpa and Uncle Earl. According to Uncle Earl, Gus-Gus was responsible for people disappearing and for "killings in the barn." "Who is this Gus-Gus guy?" C. T. muttered.

"Maybe we ought to find out," Lea said.

C. T. agreed. He grabbed the movie screen that was rolled up on the dusty floor and set it up. Then he set up the projector.

Lea found an electric outlet and plugged in the projector.

"Here goes," C. T. said, feeding the "Gus-Gus" reel into the projector.

The two of them sat on the floor as flickers of light danced across the screen in front of them. Finally a picture came into focus.

It wasn't what C. T. expected.

"What is this?" Lea asked, crinkling her brow.

Three little boys stood in the center of the screen, smiling and waving at the camera. Next to them was a pig—the biggest, fattest pig that C. T. had ever seen. The pig was wearing a blue ribbon around its neck. They were all standing under a banner that read "County Fair."

C. T. thought he recognized the boys. But before he could share his suspicions with Lea, the sound to the movie kicked in and proved that he was right.

"Hey, Luleen," the boy in the center called to someone off-camera. "Come on over here and get in the picture with me and Eddie and Ernie."

"That's Grandpa and Uncle Earl and Uncle Ernie," Lea gasped.

"And Aunt Luleen." C. T. laughed as the goofiest-looking little girl he'd ever seen waddled into the frame and pushed herself between Ernie and Earl.

"Hey, Earl," Luleen cooed, chewing on the end of one of her braids while her other hand swished the hem of her gingham skirt back and forth.

Earl lowered his head as he looked back at her and kicked at the dirt with the toe of his boot. "Are you makin' goo-goo eyes at me again, Luleen?" he said with a chuckle.

Before Luleen had a chance to answer, Ernie piped up. "She ain't makin' goo-goo eyes at you, Earl, you dumbbell. She's makin' goo-goo eyes at Hamhock here." Ernie stepped in front of the giant pig protectively. "She wants to eat him!"

"That's what pigs are for," Luleen said, sticking her tongue out at Ernie.

"You're gonna have to get past me before you go sucking on this pig's toes, Luleen," Ernie challenged.

Luleen took up the challenge, and the scene quickly faded to black as a fistfight began.

C. T. and Lea continued watching as a new scene popped up onto the screen. It looked like the same county fair. And it was definitely the same boys—Eddie, Earl, and Ernie. Only now they were standing in front of an old-fashioned arcade machine, where the player grabs a prize by moving a giant claw.

Ernie was playing.

"What on earth does this movie have to do with Gus-Gus?" Lea asked.

C. T. just shrugged. Little did he know that they were about to find out.

"I got something!" Ernie exclaimed.

C. T. and Lea watched as a red plastic egg dropped out of the claw machine into Ernie's hands.

"What is it?" Earl asked.

"Looks like an egg," Ernie answered, examining the thing.

"Open it up," Grandpa said. "I'll bet there's something inside."

Ernie popped open the egg. Sure enough, there *was* something inside. It was small, round, and furry.

"What the heck is that?" Earl asked.

"It's a gyp," Ernie complained. "It's just a fur ball. What kind of prize is this?"

C. T. and Lea watched as the thing moved in Ernie's hand.

"It's alive!" Ernie exclaimed excitedly. "Looky here! I got me a hamster or something!"

C. T. stared at the little creature in the movie. "Doesn't that thing look a lot like what we saw in the cornfield today?" he asked Lea.

Before Lea could answer, the creature in the movie jumped out of Ernie's hand onto the ground and began to roll away.

"Where's my hamster going?" Ernie cried.

The camera followed as the creature rolled into a crowd of people standing around the cow auction.

C. T. and Lea watched as a huge commotion broke out. There was screaming and yelling, people jumping around, and a whole lot of panicked mooing from the cows.

Suddenly, the picture on the screen went out of focus. C. T. and Lea couldn't see what was happening anymore.

But the sound was clear for a few more seconds. The last thing they heard was Uncle Earl's voice.

"That ain't no hamster!" Earl screamed. "That thing's a monster! He's eating Mrs. Beezley and her prize-winning cow!"

CHAPTER 10

C. T. and Lea sat staring at the blank movie screen as the end of the film flapped around and around on the reel.

Finally C. T. said, "Well, now we know who Gus-Gus is."

"You mean *what* Gus-Gus is," Lea said. "Do you really think that was what we saw out in the cornfield?"

"I'm pretty sure it was," C. T. answered. "I'll bet that's why Uncle Ernie was acting so weird, and why he wanted everybody to get out of the field."

"Do you really think there's a monster loose on this farm?" Lea practically shrieked.

"Could be." C. T. nodded.

"If that was the monster, why didn't he eat us?" Lea asked.

C. T. could tell that Lea was trying to convince herself that the monster story wasn't true. But C. T. was pretty sure that it *was*. "We were just lucky, I guess," he answered. But how long would they stay lucky?

"What are we going to do about this?" Lea asked.

C. T. didn't have an answer. And before he even had a chance to try to think of one, he heard the door to the attic open.

"Someone's coming," he whispered to Lea.

"We've got to get rid of this movie," she whispered back, trying to pull the reel off the projector. "What if it's Uncle Earl, or Uncle Ernie, or even Grandpa? We don't want them to know that we saw the movie." She got the reel free and tossed it back into the box. Then she shoved the projector back to where it had been before.

C. T. tried to get rid of the screen.

But it was too late. They were caught in the act.

"What are you two doing up here?" an angry voice demanded.

"Nothing," C. T. managed to choke out.

"You two are in big trouble," a second voice informed them.

C. T. and Lea just stood staring at the two people who confronted them, terrified of the consequences they faced. Neither one dared say a word.

A few moments of deadly silence passed before anyone spoke.

"What are we going to do with the two of you?" C. T.'s mom asked, shaking her head in exasperation.

"Your behavior has been inexcusable," Lea's mom agreed.

"But, Mom," C. T. and Lea said at the same time. Then both of them stopped talking, each one hoping the other would explain what was going on.

The moms just stood there, waiting. The expressions on their faces made it clear that no explanation was going to be acceptable.

There was another long silence.

It was C. T. who broke down first. "Something very strange is going on around here," he said.

The moms just waited, expressions unchanged.

"There's a monster on this farm," C. T. went on.

"A monster that eats people," Lea added.

At that news, both moms' expressions changed drastically. They both began to laugh.

"It's true," C. T. protested. "There's a movie to prove it. We'll show you."

"Some other time," C. T.'s mom told him. "Right now, you two are going downstairs to play with your cousins."

"Don't you understand what we're trying to tell you?" Lea said, reaching for the movie that she'd thrown back in the box.

"All I understand is that the two of you have been horribly rude," Lea's mom told her.

C. T.'s mom crossed her arms in front of her and nodded in agreement. "This is the first time the entire family has been together since you were babies. And you two haven't spent any time being nice to anybody."

"We've had it with you," Lea's mom butted in. "And so have your fathers."

"We're only going to be here for two more days," C. T.'s mom added. "I don't care how painful it is for you, you can afford to participate in family activities for two lousy days."

"And you'd better smile while you're doing it," Lea's mom warned.

"Believe me, it's no easier for us," C. T.'s mom admitted. "But a seventieth birthday is a special event. And whatever we have to do, we're going to make your grandfather happy."

"But, Mom," C. T. tried again. "You don't understand what's going on around here. We could all be in danger."

"No," his mom answered. *"You're* going to be in danger if you don't get your little butts downstairs pronto. I mean it."

"You have two minutes to put everything back the way you found it up here. Then you get downstairs and join the rest of the family," Lea's mother insisted. "Understand?"

Neither C. T. nor Lea put up more of an argument. It was useless. Their mothers were past the point of reason. C. T. and Lea both just nodded sheepishly.

"All right," C. T.'s mother said as she turned and headed back toward the stairs.

"Two minutes," Lea's mother reminded them, holding up two fingers. Then both moms left.

"I can't believe they wouldn't even listen to us," Lea complained.

"Nobody's going to listen to us," C. T. said. "It's just too weird to be true."

"But it *is* true," Lea protested. "All we have to do is get them to watch the movie." She held out the reel that was still in her hand.

Suddenly, C. T. had doubts. "What does that prove?" he asked. "All we really saw was that fur ball."

"And we heard all the screaming and hollering when it ate Mrs. Beezley and her prize-winning cow," Lea reminded him.

"But we didn't actually *see* it happen," C. T. said. "Maybe it didn't really happen. Maybe it was just some sort of joke."

"You don't really believe that, do you?" Lea asked.

C. T. didn't. But he was smart enough to know that a joke was what anybody else in the family would call the movie.

"Let's just forget about the whole thing," C. T. said to Lea, hoping that he would be able to do just that.

He took the movie reel from her hand and leaned over to put it back into the box with the rest of the movies. Then something caught his eye—something that made it clear that they were not going to be able to forget about the whole thing.

"Look at this," he said to Lea, pointing to the title of another movie in the box. "Floyd Garvey's Last Birthday Party," he read.

"Floyd Garvey?" Lea repeated the name.

"That's the guy Grandpa and Uncle Earl were arguing about," C. T. answered. "That's the guy who disappeared—because of Uncle Ernie and Gus-Gus!"

CHAPTER 11

"**W**e've got to watch this movie," C. T. insisted.

"We can't," Lea said. "Not now. If we don't get downstairs, our moms are going to have a fit."

C. T. knew that was true. And there was nothing in the world—not even the possibility of running into a monster—that scared him worse than his mom having a fit.

"Fine," he said. "But after we play nice with the Bobs and the Bobs' Twins, we'll sneak back up here and watch it."

But C. T. and Lea never got the chance to sneak back up to the attic that night. After Bobby-Bob ate one of the dice to the board game they'd been playing for hours, the adults decided that it was bedtime for everyone.

C. T. tried to sneak out of his room nearly a dozen times to get Lea and head back to the attic. But he was bunking with the Bobs, and at least one of them seemed to be awake at all times. It was as if they were taking turns keeping watch.

As he got more and more tired, C. T. began to believe that was exactly what they were doing. He began to suspect that the Bobs knew about the monster, and knew that there was danger on the farm. That was why they didn't all sleep at once. C. T. even began to believe that *everybody* knew about the monster and that they were all just keeping it a secret for some terrible reason.

As he finally dozed off, C. T. promised himself that the very next morning he and Lea were going to find out what was going on.

What C. T. didn't count on was being hauled out of bed at the very first glimmer of sunlight. Being on a farm was a lot like being in the army. The only difference was that it wasn't a bugle call that snapped everybody to attention; it was the crowing of the rooster.

The upstairs hallway was crowded with people waiting to get into the bathroom. There was no way that he and Lea could sneak up into the attic. C. T. decided that they would have to wait until after breakfast.

But even then, escape was impossible. Right after breakfast, the adults herded all the children out the door to play.

"How about a game of dodgeball?" Billy-Bob suggested.

"Good idea," Jimmy-Bob agreed.

"But we don't have a ball," Joe-Bob pointed out.

"We could use a rock," Billy-Bob said.

Bobby-Bob actually started searching the ground for a boulder.

"We've got to find a ball!" Joe-Bob yelled as he grabbed Bobby-Bob's arm.

"We've got to get out of here," C. T. whispered to Lea as the rest of them began to argue.

C. T. and Lea backed away from the group slowly until they'd reached the corner of the house. Then C. T. grabbed Lea by the shoulders, spun her around, and pushed her forward.

"Run!" he said. "As fast as you can."

They headed toward the old barn. But before they reached it, they heard the Bobs calling after them.

"C. T.! Lea!" one of the Bobs hollered.

"Where are you?" another one shouted.

"We're gonna play Stomp the Squirrel," the third Bob called excitedly.

"Stomp the Squirrel?" Lea repeated, horrified. "What on earth is that?"

"I don't know," C. T. said, not breaking stride. "And I don't want to find out. We've got to hide. In here," he said, reaching for the barn door.

"We're not allowed in the old barn. It's dangerous," Lea reminded him.

"I'll take my chances," C. T. said, ducking through the door. "Even if the whole barn falls down on our heads, it beats having to play Stomp the Squirrel, doesn't it?"

Lea was forced to agree. She followed C. T. inside and he closed the door behind them.

"Look at this place!" Lea gasped.

C. T. stood there, taking it all in, trying to make sense of what he was seeing.

The old barn wasn't falling down at all. But then, it wasn't really a barn—not inside. It looked more like a prison.

A few feet in front of them was a tall fence that crackled with electricity. The fence ran along all four walls of the barn to form a giant cage that was topped with barbed wire.

Inside the fence was a moat surrounding a small island of dirt. And on the island was yet another cage.

"What is *this* all about?" Lea asked C. T.

"How am I supposed to know?" he shot back. "This is the weirdest thing I've ever seen in my life."

C. T. inched closer to the electrified fence to get a better look at the whole creepy setup.

"Is there anything in there?" Lea asked, moving up beside him.

The cage seemed to be empty except for what looked like a cat bed in the center of it.

But when C. T. looked harder, he saw that the bed was occupied.

Lea saw it too. She jumped back, aghast.

So did C. T.

There, on the cat bed, was the fur ball named Gus-Gus.

CHAPTER 12

"That's the monster?" Lea gasped, staring into the cage at the little fur ball.

"That's him, all right," C. T. assured her.

"How did that thing eat a cow?" Lea asked.

C. T. was wondering the same thing. "Maybe he didn't. Remember, we didn't actually see it happen. Maybe it really was just a joke."

"Maybe," Lea agreed. "After all, he looks pretty harmless. He's even kind of cute and cuddly."

One thing bothered C. T. "If he's so cute and cuddly, why is he in a cage behind an electrified fence?" he wondered aloud.

Lea didn't have an answer for that one.

"And why did everybody make such a big deal about how this barn was dangerous and nobody should be inside it?" he went on.

"Do you think they all know he's in here?" Lea asked.

"If they do, then Grandma lied to us," C. T. answered. "She said she didn't know anybody named Gus-Gus."

"Grandma wouldn't lie," Lea said. "I'll bet it's only Grandpa, Uncle Earl, and Uncle Ernie who know about this."

"You're probably right," C. T. agreed. "But why are they keeping it such a big secret?"

"Because he's a monster!" Lea practically shouted.

C. T. looked at the little fur ball lying quietly in the cage and shook his head in confusion. "A monster?" he repeated. It seemed like a ridiculous idea. How could something so small be dangerous?

"Hey, Gus-Gus," C. T. called. He waited for the creature to react.

But it just lay there on its bed, motionless.

"Gus-Gus," C. T. called a little louder.

Still nothing.

"Are you sure that thing is even alive?" Lea asked.

"We saw him move before," C. T. reminded her. He picked up a pebble from the dirt floor.

"Hey, Gus-Gus," he hollered, pitching the pebble into the cage.

It missed the mark. But Gus-Gus began to move.

"He *is* alive!" Lea gasped, taking another step back.

"I wish we could get past this fence," C. T. said. "I want to have a closer look at him."

"Forget it," Lea told him. "He may look harmless, but he's in there for a reason."

C. T. was already looking for the switch that controlled the electricity.

"I'm not going to open his cage," C. T. assured her. "I just want to get closer."

C. T. found a metal box on the wall next to the barn door. But just as he opened the door to the box, the door to the barn flew open.

There was no place to run, no place to hide. C. T. knew that he and Lea had been caught. But by whom?

It took only a second to find out.

Uncle Ernie stepped into the barn, followed by Porkchop.

It was obvious that Uncle Ernie hadn't expected to find anyone else there, because when he saw C. T. and Lea a look of shock came over his face. Even Porkchop squealed in surprise.

C. T. and Lea froze in panic.

For a moment, no one spoke. They all just stared at one another.

Then Uncle Ernie turned and closed the barn door behind him. Then he bolted it shut.

"You two never should have come in here," he said. "You were warned to stay out."

"We'll get out now," C. T. told him. "And we promise we won't tell anybody what we saw."

Uncle Ernie shook his head as he stood blocking the door. "Not good enough," he told them.

"What are you going to do to us, Uncle Ernie?" C. T. asked nervously.

Uncle Ernie didn't answer him. But if looks could kill, they would have been dead on the spot.

And C. T. wasn't so sure they were going to make it out of that barn alive.

CHAPTER 13

Uncle Ernie glared at C. T. and Lea for a long moment. Then he turned his head and looked at Gus-Gus.

C. T. was terrified that Uncle Ernie was thinking about feeding them to Gus-Gus. But before C. T. could even open his mouth to plead with Uncle Ernie not to do that, Uncle Ernie started talking to himself.

"We're in a real pickle now," he muttered. "The rest of the family can't find out about this. I've got to do something with these kids—got to keep the secret. What should I do, Porkchop?" he asked his pet pig.

Porkchop cowered by the door, pawing the ground, grunting nervously.

Uncle Ernie watched him, nodding his head.

C. T. wondered what the pig was saying. Whatever it was, Uncle Ernie was listening carefully. As Porkchop kept pawing at the ground, C. T. wondered if he was suggesting that Uncle Ernie bury the two of them in the barn.

"Let us out of here!" C. T. demanded, trying to sound a lot braver than he felt.

"I can't do that," Uncle Ernie grumbled, blocking the door with his body.

"What are you going to do to us?" Lea whimpered.

"I haven't decided how to handle this yet," he answered grimly.

"Don't feed us to Gus-Gus," C. T. blurted out his worst fear.

Uncle Ernie began to laugh. "What in blazes are you talking about?" Uncle Ernie asked C. T. "You're talking crazy!"

"We know all about Gus-Gus," Lea said.

"How did you find out?" Uncle Ernie demanded. "Who told you about him?"

"Uncle Earl," C. T. answered.

"Earl!" Uncle Ernie practically roared, making Porkchop even more skittish than he already was. "There's something seriously wrong with that man. What would make him tell you about a secret we've kept for over sixty years?" Uncle Ernie didn't wait for an answer. He kept right on ranting. "Earl is a problem—a big problem. He always has been. Well, maybe it's time for me to solve that problem. Maybe I'll just feed Earl to Gus-Gus!"

"Don't do that," Lea cried. "Uncle Earl didn't exactly tell us anything. We just sort of accidentally overheard him talking to Grandpa about all kinds of creepy stuff."

"What kind of creepy stuff?" Uncle Ernie asked.

Neither one of them answered.

Uncle Ernie had another question. "Did Earl happen to mention the name Floyd Garvey?"

C. T. knew that the look on his face told Uncle Ernie that the answer was yes.

"I knew it." Uncle Ernie started to rant again. "Earl just won't let up about stupid Floyd Garvey. Floyd Garvey got exactly what was coming to him. It wasn't Gus-Gus' fault."

"What happened to Floyd Garvey?" C. T. asked nervously.

"Nothing," Ernie grumbled. But his left eye started to twitch. "It's what Floyd Garvey did to Gus-Gus that created all the problems. Gus-Gus is a good boy," he said, looking into the cage. "Aren't you, Gus-Gus?"

C. T. watched, stunned, as Gus-Gus began to roll around on his little bed, making cute, little squeaky noises as if he were answering Uncle Ernie.

"Gus-Gus," Uncle Ernie called out. "How would you like to meet two of my favorite children in the world?"

C. T. and Lea exchanged frightened glances.

"No, thanks," C. T. managed to choke out. The last thing in the world he wanted to do was take his chances with that strange little creature.

"Gus-Gus won't hurt you." Uncle Ernie laughed. "I promise."

Then he took two steps to the metal box on the wall. He threw it open and flipped a switch. The fence stopped crackling with electricity. Porkchop suddenly started squealing frantically.

Uncle Ernie flipped another switch and the gate on the fence swung open.

"Let's get out of here," C. T. cried to Lea as he started to run.

But he'd barely made it to the door when Uncle Ernie grabbed him by the shirt collar.

"No use trying to fight it," Uncle Ernie told him. "Like it or not, you're going in."

CHAPTER

14

Uncle Ernie held onto C. T.'s shirt collar as he grabbed Lea by the arm. It was no use struggling. Uncle Ernie was too strong. He marched them through the gate in the fence with great ease. Then he let go of them.

Before they could even make a move, Uncle Ernie slammed the gate shut with a loud clang. Then he used his key to lock it. Within seconds, the fence began to crackle with electricity once again. There was no hope of escape.

"Please don't do this to us, Uncle Ernie," C. T. pleaded. "We won't tell anybody else about Gus-Gus. We promise."

"Yeah, we promise," Lea echoed. "You don't have to get rid of us. Really."

"I have to make sure you never tell anyone about Gus-

Gus," Uncle Ernie insisted. "And there's only one way I can think of to do that."

Uncle Ernie picked up a wooden plank, which he put across the moat.

"Start walking," he said, shoving C. T. and Lea ahead of him.

So this was what walking the plank felt like, C. T. thought as he looked down at the murky water beneath them. The only difference was that C. T. wasn't going to fall off into the ocean to be eaten by sharks. He was stepping off onto a little island to be eaten by—he didn't know what. And he didn't know which was worse.

C. T. stopped at the end of the plank. He didn't want to step onto the island to certain death.

"Move it." Uncle Ernie shoved him again.

Both C. T. and Lea began to shake uncontrollably as they stepped onto the island where Gus-Gus lived.

"What are you so scared of?" Uncle Ernie asked them as he pulled the plank onto the island so that nobody could run away. "He really is harmless. You'll see."

"Harmless?" C. T. cried. "We saw Grandpa's movies. That thing ate a whole cow!"

Uncle Ernie didn't bother to deny it. He just shrugged. "So?"

"So?" Lea shrieked. "That's disgusting! And scary!"

Uncle Ernie just smiled and shook his head. "Let me ask you a question," he said. "Do you eat hamburgers?"

Both C. T. and Lea nodded as they exchanged confused looks. Where was Uncle Ernie going with this?

"Then you eat cows too," he explained. "So you can't fault Gus-Gus for that. After all, he's not scared of you because you eat cows. Are you, Gus-Gus?"

Gus-Gus answered with more little squeaky noises as he began rolling toward his cage door.

"Besides," Ernie went on, "I don't let Gus-Gus eat meat anymore. It's bad for him—*very* bad."

"So what does he eat now?" C. T. asked.

Uncle Ernie didn't answer. Instead, he reached into his pocket and pulled out a key. He stuck it into the lock on the cage door and turned it.

C. T. was ready to dive into the moat and swim for the other side. It was only a few feet, after all. It's not like he'd have any problem making it. But once he got to the other side, he was still stuck. The fence was electrified and the key was in Uncle Ernie's pocket.

There was nothing to do but hope that Uncle Ernie wasn't lying to them—hope that Gus-Gus really was as harmless as he looked. C. T. tried hard to swallow his fear, but it stuck in his throat in a knot so big he could barely breathe.

Lea let out a small cry when Uncle Ernie threw open the door to the cage.

"Come on out and say hello to Catan Thomas and Lea Rose, Gus-Gus," he said as he stepped aside to clear the way.

Lea jumped behind C. T. and held onto his shoulders. If somebody was going to get eaten, C. T. was going to be first.

Gus-Gus was still for a moment. Then, without warning, he rolled toward C. T. with lightning speed.

Before C. T. had a chance to jump out of the way, Gus-Gus grabbed onto his ankle and held fast.

C. T. screamed in terror as he felt the first pinch of what felt like razor-sharp fangs.

CHAPTER 15

"*Aaaaaaaagggggggggghhhhhh!*" C. T. continued to scream as the pinching sensation moved up his body. His eyes were closed tight. He didn't want to see what was happening to him.

Then something touched his nose—something cold and wet.

C. T. waited for his face to be ripped off.

His eyes popped open in horror.

"Calm down," Uncle Ernie shouted.

But C. T. could barely hear him over the sound of his own screaming.

C. T. was so terrified that it took his brain a full minute to realize what his eyes were looking at.

It was Gus-Gus all right. But he wasn't a fur ball anymore.

C. T. finally stopped screaming. He blinked hard to

make sure he was seeing correctly, then just stared.

Gus-Gus stared back at him with small, black beady eyes.

"What is he?" C. T. gasped to Uncle Ernie.

Uncle Ernie shrugged. "Nobody knows exactly. He's a strange little critter, isn't he?"

Strange wasn't the word for it.

Gus-Gus was hanging onto C. T.'s collar with a pair of leathery-looking claws. His hind feet were braced against C. T.'s chest. Gus-Gus wasn't rolled into a ball anymore—he was all stretched out.

Only Gus-Gus' back and the top of his head were furry. His underside was leathery. His face looked like the face of a bat, and he had bat ears.

"Get him off me!" C. T. said through clenched teeth.

"Why?" Uncle Ernie asked. "He likes you. Don't you, Gus-Gus?"

Gus-Gus let out a little squeak and rubbed his nose against C. T. It was the same cold, wet feeling as before.

"He does seem to like you," Lea said, sounding amazed.

Then Gus-Gus started moving.

"What's he doing now?" C. T. cried.

"He's just going to curl up on your shoulder," Uncle Ernie said calmly. "That's where he likes to sit."

C. T. stood perfectly still as Gus-Gus did exactly what Uncle Ernie said he would. When he got onto C. T.'s shoulder, he curled back into a little fur ball and made a contented cooing sound.

"I told you Gus-Gus was a good boy," Uncle Ernie said, patting the creature gently. "Why don't you pet him?" he suggested to Lea. "He's soft."

Lea hesitated for a moment. Then, slowly and cautiously, she stepped toward C. T. and reached out her hand. At first, only her fingertips touched Gus-Gus.

"He really is soft," she told C. T. as she began to pet Gus-Gus a little more boldly.

Gus-Gus began to coo again.

"See," Uncle Ernie said, smiling. "Gus-Gus really is nothing to be afraid of."

C. T. wasn't convinced. "Then how come Grandpa and Uncle Earl were arguing about you and Gus-Gus?" he asked Uncle Ernie.

"Because Earl's a raving maniac," Uncle Ernie answered. "He's been holding a grudge against me and Gus-Gus for sixty years. All because of Floyd Garvey."

Floyd Garvey. There was that name again.

"Uncle Earl said that Floyd Garvey disappeared," Lea said to Uncle Ernie. She stopped petting Gus-Gus and began to step back, away from him.

C. T.'s body began to tense again as he looked at the little fur ball on his shoulder.

"Floyd Garvey ran off and joined the circus," Uncle Ernie told them, covering his left eye. "But that knucklehead Earl thinks that Gus-Gus ate him."

Now C. T. was really tense. "What would make Uncle Earl think that?"

"It all started at Floyd Garvey's twelfth birthday party,"

Uncle Ernie answered. "Now, granted, I should never have brought Gus-Gus along in the first place. But Floyd Garvey and the other kids already knew about him. Most of those kids were at the county fair when I got Gus-Gus."

"The county fair where Gus-Gus ate Mrs. Beezley and her cow?" Lea asked nervously.

"The county fair where Hamhock won the blue ribbon," Uncle Earl said, avoiding the question.

C. T. really wanted Gus-Gus off his shoulder now, but he was too afraid to try. "Uncle Ernie," he said, "can you put Gus-Gus back in his cage now?"

"After I explain about Floyd Garvey," Uncle Ernie told him. "Now, where was I?" Uncle Ernie scratched his head, thinking—which was hard for Uncle Ernie to do. "I know," he said, answering his own question. "I was at Floyd Garvey's birthday party." His left eye suddenly calmed down. "Now Floyd Garvey knew that Gus-Gus was not allowed to have meat. But Floyd Garvey didn't care about that. Floyd Garvey just kept feeding Gus-Gus pieces of fried chicken so that he could watch Gus-Gus grow bigger and bigger."

C. T. remembered how big Gus-Gus had been the first time he saw him out in the cornfield. He also remembered that Bobby-Bob had said he saw Gus-Gus eat a field mouse and grow right before his eyes.

"Does Gus-Gus grow every time he eats?" Lea asked.

"Only when he eats meat," Uncle Ernie answered. "And you can't imagine how big he can get, or just how much he can eat. Anyway, to finish my story, Floyd Garvey ran out of fried chicken long before Gus-Gus ran out of appetite."

"What happened then?" C. T. wanted to know.

"Well," Earl went on, "Gus-Gus and Floyd Garvey got into a little bit of a scuffle, which scared Earl half to death. But Gus-Gus did not eat Floyd Garvey." He covered his eye again. "Floyd Garvey escaped with hardly a scratch on him. And then he ran off and joined the circus. So you two just forget all about what Earl said. Okay?"

C. T. and Lea both nodded. But they also shot each other looks of disbelief.

Aside from the fact that Uncle Ernie's eye was all aflutter, his story sounded pretty fishy.

"Now that we've put that to rest, it's time to feed Gus-Gus," Uncle Ernie said.

C. T. gulped. "Feed Gus-Gus?" he repeated nervously, looking at the little creature perched on his shoulder.

"What exactly does Gus-Gus eat now?" Lea asked, backing up all the way to the water's edge.

C. T.'s eyes scanned the barn for anything that looked like food.

He saw Porkchop still cowering beside the barn door on the other side of the electrified fence. But he knew there was no way Uncle Ernie was going to feed his pet pig and favorite companion to the monster. No, C. T. was sure that he and Lea were about to become monster chow.

"Are you hungry, Gus-Gus?" Uncle Ernie asked with a grin.

The monster skittered down C. T.'s body as quickly as it had climbed up.

When he got to the floor, he uncurled his body, stood up on his hind legs, and let out a ferocious growl that echoed off the walls.

Breakfast was about to be served!

CHAPTER 16

"No!" C. T. screamed, moving in front of Lea to protect her. "Don't let him eat us!"

"There you go acting crazy again," Uncle Ernie said. "How many times do I have to tell you that Gus-Gus will not hurt you as long as you treat him right." He reached into his pocket and pulled out a jar of baby food. "This is what Gus-Gus eats now."

"Baby food?" C. T. gasped. "A monster that eats baby food?" That was impossible.

"Sweet potatoes." Uncle Ernie held up the jar for them to see. "That's his very favorite. I make sure to give him sweet potatoes at least once a day."

Gus-Gus curled into a ball again and rolled into his cage to the food bowl that was hidden in the corner. He moved so quickly that he was almost a blur. When he got to his food bowl, he stood up and growled.

"I'd better get to it," Uncle Ernie said, popping the lid off the jar as he rushed over to dump the contents into the bowl.

Gus-Gus began slurping it up even before the jar was emptied.

"How many times a day does he eat?" C. T. asked, watching Gus-Gus curiously.

"Every two or three hours," Uncle Ernie answered as he straightened up with the empty jar in his hand. "As long as I keep him well fed, he's happy, and he's quiet, and he won't bother anybody."

"Every two or three hours?" Lea said. "That must be a real pain."

"You bet it is," Uncle Ernie assured her. "Especially in the middle of the night. But if Gus-Gus doesn't get fed regularly, there'll be the chickens to pay."

"Chickens?" C. T. gulped.

"Did I say chickens?" Uncle Ernie laughed and twitched. "I meant dickens," he corrected himself. "There'll be the dickens to pay."

C. T. shot Lea a look as Uncle Ernie came out of the cage, leaving Gus-Gus to eat. Then Uncle Ernie closed the door behind him and locked it up.

"Why do you keep him?" C. T. asked.

Uncle Ernie had a simple answer for that. "I can't get rid of him," he said.

"What do you mean, you can't get rid of him?" C. T. asked.

"Just what I said," Uncle Ernie shot back. "Gus-Gus has been around for over sixty years—and probably a whole lot longer than that. You can't kill him. And you can't lose him. Eddie and Earl have tried over and over again. One time they drove for days. They finally tossed him into a lake in the middle of nowhere with a cement block tied around his neck. But, sure enough, Gus-Gus made it back home even before they did. And that time, he was bigger, and badder, and meaner than I've ever seen him."

"What did he do?" C. T. asked.

"You don't want to know." Uncle Ernie dismissed the question with a wave of his hand. Then he bent down to put the plank back across the moat. "Time to go," he told them. "After Gus-Gus eats he likes to have a nap." He stepped aside and waited for Lea and C. T. to walk the plank back to the other side.

Lea went first and she went fast, relieved to be going.

But C. T. paused before he started across to ask Uncle Ernie yet another question. "Does he like to have a nap after he eats meat?"

Uncle Ernie shook his head. "Trust me, you don't want to meet up with Gus-Gus after he's had a taste of flesh."

C. T. shivered at the thought.

"Don't worry about it," Uncle Ernie said, patting him on the shoulder. "I keep him on a strict diet. And as long as nobody interferes with that, Gus-Gus is nothing but a cute little critter."

C. T. wanted to believe that. He wanted to believe that Uncle Ernie had the situation under control and that no one on the farm was in danger. But that was a real leap of faith—especially since he'd overheard Uncle Earl talk about "disappearances" and "killings in the barn." He shot one last look at Gus-Gus before Uncle Ernie moved him onto the plank and nudged him across.

When they got to the other side, Uncle Ernie pulled the plank across again. Then he took out his key, turned off the electricity in the fence, and opened the gate.

Without another word, they all went out the gate and Uncle Ernie reactivated it. Gus-Gus was securely behind bars—electrified, barbed-wire-topped bars.

"Now," Uncle Ernie said, "you've got to promise me that you won't talk about Gus-Gus to anyone."

Neither C. T. nor Lea said anything. Both of them just looked across the moat into the cage where Gus-Gus was still lapping up his jar of baby food. For a monster, he sure did eat slowly. C. T. couldn't figure it out.

"Promise?" Uncle Ernie urged them.

They both nodded.

"We promise," C. T. said.

Who were they going to tell, after all? What could anybody do about it anyway?

"Gus-Gus is my responsibility," Uncle Ernie said very seriously. "I'm the one who got him, and I'm the one who's stuck with him. I take good care of him. Earl's the one who causes all the problems. I have to keep Earl away from Gus-Gus, because Earl does nothing but provoke him and make him nasty. You understand?"

"Yeah," C. T. answered. "We're not supposed to talk to

Uncle Earl about this." As if C. T. wanted to talk to Uncle Earl or any of his kin about anything.

"And don't tell anybody else either," Uncle Ernie stressed. He opened the barn door and Porkchop shot out like a bullet. "And don't get any ideas about going to visit Gus-Gus without me," Uncle Ernie went on. "He's a smart little bugger. And if you don't take the necessary precautions, he'll sneak right past you. He did it to me just the other morning when I was too lazy to pull up the plank and electrify the fence. Luckily I managed to catch him in the cornfield before he got too out of control."

"Don't worry Uncle Ernie," C. T. assured him. "We won't be visiting."

Lea stepped outside, followed by C. T. Uncle Ernie came out last, closing the barn door behind him.

"I ought to put a lock on this door," he said. "With so many people around here this weekend, you never know what might happen."

"That's probably a good idea, Uncle Ernie," C. T. agreed. "You don't want anybody else getting in there to find Gus-Gus."

But even as the three of them followed Porkchop away from the barn and back toward the house, somebody else was listening—*lots* of somebody elses.

CHAPTER 17

When C. T. and Lea got back to the house with Uncle Ernie, they found a flurry of activity. Everyone was busy getting things ready for Grandpa's big birthday celebration that night.

It was going to be a huge party. Not only was the whole family going to be there, a lot of people from town were coming too.

C. T.'s and Lea's fathers, and Billy-Bob, Sr., were busy setting up tables and chairs on the lawn, while the women were in the kitchen preparing enormous amounts of food.

The Bobs and the Bobs' Twins were nowhere to be seen. Neither were Grandpa and Uncle Earl.

"Where'd Eddie and Earl go?" Uncle Ernie asked Grandma as he dipped a finger into the cake batter she was whipping up.

"Earl took Eddie for a ride into town," Grandma answered. "He's going to keep him busy all day so we can set everything up and surprise him when he gets back."

"I thought Grandpa knew that we were having a birthday party for him," C. T. said to Grandma.

"He knew the whole family was here to celebrate his birthday," Grandma explained. "But he didn't know that we were having such a big party and inviting other people too. That part is the surprise."

It was a surprise to C. T. too—and a nightmare. It was bad enough having to put up with family members, but having to be nice to a bunch of strangers from Bumbleweed was just too much to take.

"Why don't you two go outside and help decorate," C. T.'s mom said to C. T. and Lea.

"You too, Ernie," Grandma said, slapping his hand as he stuck his finger into her batter again.

The three of them headed toward the door obediently as the work in the kitchen continued.

"Where are all my sweet grandbabies?" Aunt Luleen called after them. She was up to her elbows in pickled pig parts.

"Haven't seen 'em," Uncle Ernie answered.

"Neither have we," C. T. said. Then he and Lea beat it out the door before Aunt Luleen asked any more questions. They didn't want to be forced to admit that they'd ditched the Bobs and the Bobs' Twins long ago.

Uncle Ernie headed right off the porch and started pitching in with the rest of the men. But C. T. grabbed

Lea and ducked around the side of the house.

"Where are we going?" Lea protested.

"Just follow me," C. T. said as he dragged her around to the front. Then he motioned her to be quiet and peeked in the front window. When C. T. saw that the coast was clear, he opened the front door.

"We're going to sneak back to the attic and watch the Floyd Garvey movie," he whispered, letting Lea in on his plan. "Nobody will miss us."

The two of them slipped through the door, and crept up the stairs to the second floor.

As they started toward the attic door, Lea whispered, "Why do you want to watch the Floyd Garvey movie now? Uncle Ernie's already told us all about Floyd Garvey."

C. T. stopped and looked Lea in the eye. "Do you really believe him?"

Lea shrugged.

"Me neither," C. T. said. "I want to see for myself."

The two of them headed up the attic stairs.

"You set up the movie screen," he told Lea. "I'll set up the projector."

The Floyd Garvey movie was right on top, just as they'd left it. C. T. took it to the projector and began to feed it in. As he got the picture focused on the screen, Lea sat down beside him on the floor.

The picture that popped up on the screen was a birthday party—a really goofy birthday party.

"I can't believe that a bunch of twelve-year-olds are

running around wearing party hats." Lea laughed at the scene.

C. T. laughed too. "I guess kids didn't worry about looking nerdy back then."

"Look!" Lea cried, pointing at the screen. "There's Grandpa and Uncle Earl and Uncle Ernie."

The camera panned in on each one of them sitting at the table. It stopped on Uncle Ernie as he reached into his pocket with one hand while gesturing with the other hand for everybody to wait a minute.

"Whatcha got there, Ernie?" Floyd Garvey asked.

C. T. and Lea could tell it was Floyd Garvey because his party hat said "Birthday Boy" on it.

"You'll see," Uncle Ernie said. Then he pulled Gus-Gus out of his pocket and set him down on the table.

"Have you figured out what this thing is yet?" one of the other boys at the party asked.

"Yeah," Uncle Earl answered. "It's some kind of monster."

Everybody laughed at Uncle Earl—everybody but Grandpa.

"Give him here," Floyd Garvey said, scooping Gus-Gus up.

Gus-Gus started licking Floyd Garvey's fingers.

Floyd Garvey started laughing. "Hey, you're tickling me," he said to Gus-Gus.

Gus-Gus kept right on licking.

"Why are you doing that?" Floyd Garvey asked the little creature, as if he might answer.

"Uh-oh," Uncle Ernie said. "You'd better give him back to me."

"Why?" Floyd Garvey asked, keeping Gus-Gus to himself.

"Because you've been eating fried chicken," Uncle Ernie answered. "Gus-Gus tastes it on your fingers. That's why he's licking them. That's a big problem."

"So he's hungry," Floyd Garvey said. "That's not a problem. There's plenty of fried chicken left."

Before Uncle Ernie could stop him, Floyd Garvey gave Gus-Gus a piece of fried chicken.

He gobbled it down much more quickly than he'd eaten the baby food.

"This is exactly what Uncle Ernie said happened," Lea told C. T.

But C. T. was sure that something else was going to happen—something that Uncle Ernie *hadn't* told them about. "Let's just keep watching," he said to Lea, his eyes glued to the screen.

"Don't do that!" Uncle Ernie cried.

But Floyd Garvey gave Gus-Gus another piece of chicken.

He gobbled that up too, and immediately doubled in size.

"Stop!" Uncle Ernie shouted.

But it was too late. Floyd Garvey had already given Gus-Gus another piece.

By the time Uncle Ernie made it out of his seat and around the table to stop Floyd Garvey from feeding Gus-Gus, the whole plate of fried chicken was gone. And Gus-

Gus wanted more.

For the first time, C. T. and Lea saw with their own eyes the monster Gus-Gus really was. It was a pretty terrifying sight.

The Gus-Gus they saw on the movie screen had grown from a little fur ball to a creature twice as big as any of the children at Floyd Garvey's birthday party. He was standing on his hind legs. The front of him was all muscular and leathery. But his face was particularly scary.

Gus-Gus' beady eyes were as big as softballs. They stared right at Floyd Garvey as his mouth hung open like a shark's. His razor-sharp teeth looked to be at least two inches long.

Gus-Gus wanted more chicken. But there was none left. Gus-Gus lunged for Floyd Garvey.

Lea covered her eyes.

C. T. wanted to cover his eyes too, but he had to know what happened next.

Floyd Garvey got up from his chair and tried to run, but he fell. Gus-Gus flung himself down on top of the boy. The camera went out of focus trying to follow the scuffle.

C. T. couldn't make out what anyone at the party was saying. Everybody was screaming hysterically.

Then suddenly, something unexpected happened.

Something terrible. Something that made C. T. scream.

CHAPTER

18

"What's going on?" C. T. cried.

Lea peeked through the fingers that were covering her eyes.

The movie had stopped dead. There was nothing on the screen. No light was coming from the projector, and the reel wasn't moving. The light bulb dangling from the ceiling had gone out too.

"It looks like there was a power failure," Lea said, lowering her hands.

C. T. flipped the projector switch on and off several times. Nothing happened. Lea was probably right. There had been a power failure.

It couldn't have happened at a worse time. They were just about to find out what really happened to Floyd Garvey.

"What do you think caused it?" Lea asked. "It's not like there's a storm or anything."

"I don't know." C. T. shrugged. "Maybe a fuse blew or something."

"Let's go downstairs and find out," Lea suggested, getting to her feet.

"No way," C. T. told her. "If we go down there and all those goofy cousins are around, we'll never be able to get back up here to finish watching this movie. I say we stay put until the power comes back on."

"And what are we supposed to do up here in the meantime?" Lea said, pacing back and forth.

"Wait," C. T. answered impatiently.

He moved over to the box marked "Grandpa's Monster Movies" and began digging through it again, looking for anything else that might relate to Gus-Gus. Lea looked out the window.

"Uh, C. T., you might want to take a look at this," she suggested.

"Why? What is it?" he asked, not bothering to get up.

"You have to see for yourself," she insisted.

C. T. pulled himself to his feet and shuffled toward the window.

"Hurry up!" Lea said. "I think I know what caused the power failure!"

C. T. looked out the window.

He couldn't believe what he saw.

"The Bobs!" he exclaimed, horrified.

Billy-Bob, Joe-Bob, and Jimmy-Bob were all dancing around in front of the old barn door as if their pants were on fire.

"They came running out of there one by one," Lea told C. T.

One of the twins came running out of the barn, screaming her head off.

"Which one is that?" C. T. asked. "April or May?"

"Who knows," Lea answered. "Who cares?"

"It looks like they've found out about Gus-Gus," C. T. said.

"Yeah," Lea agreed. "The hard way."

Then Bobby-Bob staggered out the barn door after his brothers and sister.

Bobby-Bob was in pretty bad shape. It looked like his pants really were on fire, because smoke was billowing up from them. His face and hands were charred and the hair on his head was standing straight up in the air.

"What the heck happened to him?" C. T. asked.

"Something tells me he touched the electrified fence," Lea said.

"No," C. T. gasped. He couldn't believe that anybody would be that stupid. But then he remembered they were talking about Bobby-Bob. "What a noodle-head," he said to himself.

"I'll bet you anything they caused the power failure," Lea said.

Of course. That was exactly what had to have happened.

Then a terrible thought occurred to C. T. "If there's no electricity . . ."

He didn't have time to finish his thought before it proved itself to be true. Without the electrified fence to hold him back, Gus-Gus had managed to get free.

C. T. and Lea watched in horror as the little fur ball rolled out of the barn and the Bobs and the lone Bobs' Twin ran screaming in all directions.

CHAPTER 19

"We'd better get out there and see what's going on," C. T. said as everybody—including Gus-Gus—disappeared from sight.

Without another word, C. T. and Lea dashed away from the window, down the attic steps, through the hallway, and down the stairs.

If C. T. had been thinking clearly, he would have gone out the front door. But he wasn't. He wanted to get to the barn as quickly as possible, and it was quicker to go out the back door than all the way around the house. So he ran for the kitchen—and right *smack* into Aunt Luleen.

"Whoa," she said, grabbing him by the shoulders as Lea pulled up short behind him. "What kind of manners is that?" she reprimanded. "You should know better than to run inside the house. If you want to run around like that, you go outside."

"Sorry, Aunt Luleen," C. T. hurriedly apologized. "We'll go outside right now."

Aunt Luleen let go and C. T. started for the door as quickly as he could make his legs move without actually running. Lea kept pace.

"Not so fast," Grandma snagged them. "I've got a job for the two of you."

C. T. didn't even have time to try to think up an excuse before his mother butted in.

"It's about time the two of you did something to help out," she said firmly.

Lea caved in first. "What do you want us to do, Grandma?" she asked, trying to sound helpful.

Grandma reached into a cabinet and handed her a basket with a handle on it. "I want the two of you to go out to the henhouse and collect a dozen eggs for me," she instructed. "I need the egg whites to make the icing for Grandpa's birthday cake."

"Okay," Lea said.

"And don't dawdle," Grandma said, shaking a finger at them. "I need those eggs right away."

"We'll be back in a flash," C. T. assured her. He wanted to get this job out of the way as quickly as possible so he could turn his attention to the problem at hand—namely, the monster that was running loose on the farm.

C. T. practically pushed Lea out the back door. "Come on," he said, leaping off the porch without bothering to use the steps. "Let's move it!"

The men were still setting up tables and decorations

on the back lawn for the big party.

"Where are you two headed so fast?" C. T.'s father called to them as he worked on lighting the barbecue.

"We've got to collect some eggs for Grandma," C. T. answered, not breaking stride as he ran in the direction of the henhouse. It was in the opposite direction from the old barn, which was where he really wanted to go. But that would have to wait.

Then a thought occurred to C. T. He stopped so quickly that Lea ran right past him. "Hey, Dad," he called back to his father. "Where's Uncle Ernie?" C. T. figured that Uncle Ernie should know that Gus-Gus was loose. Maybe Uncle Ernie could do something about it.

"I don't know," C. T.'s dad answered. "He and Porkchop wandered off quite a while ago."

"C. T. , come on," Lea hollered at him. "We've got to get Grandma's eggs before we do anything else or we'll be in big trouble."

C. T. knew she was right. There was no way the two of them could tell anybody about the monster. Nobody would believe them. And C. T. had the horrible feeling that Uncle Ernie, Uncle Earl, and even Grandpa wouldn't back up their story. For some reason, the three brothers had kept the secret from the rest of the family. They weren't about to confess now.

C. T. ran to catch up with Lea.

Luckily, the henhouse wasn't far from the house. None of the important buildings were.

"Do you have any idea how we're supposed to get

these eggs?" Lea asked C. T. as they stood outside the henhouse door.

C. T. didn't. The only place he'd ever gotten eggs was the supermarket. "Beats me," he said. "I think we're supposed to reach under the chickens and take the eggs out of the nest."

As C. T. moved to open the door, Lea stopped him. "That sounds totally mean," she said, grimacing. "Aren't those eggs supposed to be their babies?"

"I don't know," C. T. said, grossed out by the thought. "And I don't want to know. Look, farmers collect eggs every day, so it must not upset the chickens too much."

"What if they get mad?" Lea asked. "What if they try to bite us or something?"

"Oh geez," C. T. muttered. He'd never thought of that. Once again, he wished they'd never come to Bumbleweed. "We'll deal with it," he answered, reaching for the door again. "It can't be that hard to collect eggs," he told Lea. "It's not like Grandma would send us on a life or death mission."

Lea stood aside so that C. T. could open the door.

The first thing C. T. noticed, even before he'd stepped inside, was a horrible squawking.

"What's going on in there?" Lea asked as she followed C. T. into the henhouse.

He didn't answer. In fact, neither one of them spoke. The scene that confronted them was too terrible for words.

CHAPTER 20

C. T. and Lea were not going to be able to collect the eggs that Grandma wanted.

There were no eggs—because there were no chickens!

Well, there was one chicken. But something was terribly wrong with it.

The poor thing was screaming its head off.

C. T. and Lea never would have seen it otherwise, because it was perched on the rafters high above their heads.

C. T. couldn't imagine how a chicken—a flightless bird—had gotten way up there. But more strange than that was the chicken's appearance.

It had no feathers.

"Something's really wrong," Lea said finally, stating the obvious. "What happened to all the chickens?"

"How should I know?" C. T. answered. But he did know. Deep down inside, he knew exactly what had happened in that henhouse. Especially when he remembered Uncle Ernie's earlier slip of the tongue.

There'll be the chickens to pay, Uncle Ernie's voice echoed in his head.

C. T. cringed. He refused to believe what he knew was the truth.

But Lea knew it too. And she was daring enough to say it out loud. "Do you think Gus-Gus did this?" She looked at C. T. with terror in her eyes.

"No way!" he lied—to himself and to Lea.

Something skittered across the floor against the far wall. The unexpected movement made both C. T. and Lea jump.

"What was that?" Lea shrieked.

"I don't know," C. T. answered, his eyes darting around the henhouse looking for any sign of movement.

From the rafters above them, the one last chicken began squawking even more frantically. It was looking at something on the ground.

C. T.'s eyes moved to the far corner of the henhouse where the chicken's attention was focused. At first all he saw were a few bales of hay stacked up near the wall. But then he saw the same movement on the ground that he had seen before.

"Look," he whispered, pointing it out to Lea.

"It's just a shadow," she told him.

"A shadow of what?" he asked nervously.

The answer came as the shadow began to move out from behind the bales of hay. It was a huge shadow—a monstrous shadow—but it was nowhere near as terrifying as the body that created it.

"It's Gus-Gus!" C. T. cried, staring at the monster that confronted them.

Gus-Gus, standing on his hind legs, was well over six feet tall. There was nothing cute about him anymore. The hair on his back and on the top of his head didn't look soft and furry. It looked more like porcupine quills. His enormous, leathery claws looked deadly as he slashed at the air, ready to strike.

His bat's face was truly hideous. His mouth was open wide enough to reveal long, razor-sharp teeth.

For a moment, C. T. was too panic-stricken to move. He'd seen the lightning speed with which Gus-Gus could move. And he was afraid that any movement from the two of them might provoke him.

"We've got to get out of here!" Lea screamed, grabbing C. T.'s arm and pulling him toward the door.

C. T. didn't dare take his eyes off Gus-Gus. As he ran for the door with Lea, he watched over his shoulder for any sign that Gus-Gus would attack them.

Gus-Gus watched them intently, licking his chops hungrily, but he made no move—until they'd made it to the door. Then Gus-Gus opened his mouth wide and let out the biggest, grossest burp that C. T. had ever heard.

As the monster burped, a cloud of feathers escaped from his mouth—feathers and something else.

C. T. caught only a glimpse of the other object before he darted out the door after Lea. But a glimpse was all he needed.

Gus-Gus had eaten more than chickens. What had come out of his mouth with the feathers was a pink gingham bow—the same kind of bow that the Bobs' Twins wore in their hair.

CHAPTER 21

"Oh, no!" Lea cried as they slammed the door to the henhouse, trapping Gus-Gus inside.

"What's the matter?" C. T. asked.

"We can't just leave that poor little chicken in there with the monster," Lea explained in a voice full of panic and horror. "She'll get eaten for sure!"

"Well, I'm not going back in there," C. T. said.

The squawking coming from inside grew louder. Then it stopped.

C. T. could only guess what had happened.

"This is too terrible," Lea said, sounding on the verge of tears.

"You don't know the half of it," C. T. said, almost afraid to tell her. But he had to. "I think Gus-Gus ate one of the Bobs' Twins," he blurted out.

"What makes you think that?" Lea asked.

"I saw him burp up one of their bows," he answered.

"Who do you think it was?" Lea shrieked in horror. "April or May?"

"How should I know!" C. T. shot back. But for the first time, he actually cared.

"Oh, man," Lea cried. "We'd better get out of here! If that monster ate one of the twins, what's to keep him from eating us?" Lea started to run. "We've got to tell everybody about this."

C. T. quickly caught up with Lea and stopped her. He was sure that no one would believe them, and in the time it took to convince them, who knew what damage Gus-Gus could do. Besides, what could any of the adults at the house do to stop the monster?

There was only one person who had any idea what to do. "We've got to find Uncle Ernie," C. T. told Lea. "He's the only one who can handle this."

Lea nodded her head. Then panic took hold again. "But we don't know where Uncle Ernie is!"

"We'll find him," C. T. insisted, trying to stay calm.

"This farm is hundreds of acres," Lea shrieked. "Where are we supposed to start looking?"

C. T. looked back toward the henhouse. Gus-Gus hadn't come out and there was no sign that he was planning to. Maybe he was taking a nap. C. T. remembered Uncle Ernie telling them that Gus-Gus liked to nap after he'd eaten. And he certainly had eaten. With any luck, he'd be sleeping it off for a long time, and C. T. and Lea would have time to find Uncle Ernie.

But where should they start looking?

"The cornfield," C. T. said, pulling Lea along quickly in that direction. "Porkchop likes to take walks in the cornfield because Uncle Ernie tosses him a couple of ears of corn along the way."

"But what if Gus-Gus follows us out to the cornfield, and Uncle Ernie isn't out there?" Lea asked. "What happens to us then?"

C. T. refused to think about that. If Uncle Ernie didn't get this situation under control right away, something terrible would happen to the whole family. "What a crummy time for Grandpa and Uncle Earl to be gone," C. T. lamented.

"What a crummy birthday present this is going to be for Grandpa," Lea said. "He'll come home and find his whole family eaten by a monster."

"That's not going to happen," C. T. insisted. "Maybe I was wrong about the Bobs' Twin's bow. Maybe it was just a pink chicken feather or something. And maybe everything will be all fixed before Grandpa gets back. Maybe he'll never even have to find out about it."

The cornfield was just up ahead. "Uncle Ernie! Uncle Ernie!" C. T. began to shout.

Lea joined in.

There was no answer.

"I'm not going in there," Lea said, stopping at the edge of the field where the tall stalks began.

"Then I'll go in by myself," C. T. said. "You wait here."

Lea grabbed hold of his shirt. "No way!" she told him.

"We are not splitting up. Let's just walk along the edge of the field and keep hollering for him."

C. T. was forced to give in.

They began the long walk down the edge of the field, hollering for Uncle Ernie until they were both hoarse. C. T. was about to give up and try to think of another place to look for him when he heard the rustle of cornstalks.

"Uncle Ernie?" he shouted with everything that was left of his voice.

There was no answer except the sound of stalks beginning to crack.

C. T. had a bad feeling. "Uncle Ernie? Is that you?"

No answer.

"Run!" Lea screamed as she took off.

C. T. didn't get a chance to follow.

The cornstalks directly in front of him parted. Before C. T. knew what hit him, he was knocked to the ground—just like Floyd Garvey.

CHAPTER 22

C. T. was sure he was dead. He just hoped it would all be over quickly and painlessly.

But the monster that had C. T. pinned to the ground didn't eat him. He just snorted and drooled in C. T.'s face as he pressed his nose against C. T.'s.

"Porkchop!" C. T. hollered, when he finally realized that it was only Uncle Ernie's pig that had attacked him.

Porkchop nuzzled C. T. affectionately.

"Get off me, you stupid pig!" C. T. struggled with all his might to get out from under the beast.

It was useless. Even though Aunt Luleen called Porkchop a runt, he still weighed a couple hundred pounds. It was impossible to move him if he didn't want to move. He kept on nuzzling C. T.

"Porkchop," Uncle Ernie said, stepping out of the cornfield. "Get off that boy right now."

Porkchop obeyed, snorting apologetically as he backed off.

"Uncle Ernie," Lea cried, running toward him.

C. T. pulled himself to his feet. "Gus-Gus is loose," he shouted.

"No." Uncle Ernie shook his head as if he refused to believe it.

"He is," Lea said. "And it's bad, Uncle Ernie. He's eaten all the chickens in the henhouse."

Uncle Ernie just kept shaking his head. "This can't be happening. How did he get loose? Did you kids go back into that barn after I was gone?"

"No," C. T. told him. "It wasn't us. It was the Bobs and the Bobs' Twins who let him out. And you haven't heard the worst of it. I think Gus-Gus may have eaten one of the twins."

"Can't be," Uncle Ernie said. "Can't be," he repeated. "That's the one thing I can count on from Gus-Gus. He will not eat family members."

C. T. watched Uncle Ernie's left eye carefully. But this time it wasn't twitching.

"We've got to do something," Lea said. "We've got to stop him."

"You're right about that," Uncle Ernie said. "Where was he when you saw him last?"

"In the henhouse," C. T. answered.

"Okay," Uncle Ernie said. "Let's go." He started running.

C. T. and Lea followed. Porkchop brought up the rear, grunting nervously as he trotted along behind them.

"What are you going to do when you catch him?" C. T. wanted to know.

"I've got to trick him into taking a tranquilizer," Uncle Ernie answered. "It will put him to sleep for a while, so I can get him back into his cage." Uncle Ernie began to pant from the exertion of running. "Then everything will be all right. Trust me. We've got to go to the barn first to get the tranquilizer. Then we've got to find some meat to hide it in—something Gus-Gus will want to eat."

"How about one of Aunt Luleen's pig's feet?" C. T. suggested.

"Good thinking," Uncle Ernie said as Porkchop squealed in horror. "Sorry, Porkchop," Uncle Ernie said over his shoulder. "But you know how Gus-Gus loves pork."

The henhouse was just a few hundred yards ahead of them. But instead of heading straight for it, Uncle Ernie turned toward the old barn.

"Why don't you kids go straight to the house and grab a couple of Luleen's pig's feet," Uncle Ernie said. "It will save us some time."

"We can't," Lea said. "If Grandma sees us, she's going to want to know why we didn't bring her the eggs she wanted. Then what are we supposed to tell her?"

"All right," Uncle Ernie said. "I'll go grab the feet. You two meet me at the barn."

Uncle Ernie took off toward the house with Porkchop still lagging behind him. C. T. and Lea stopped running and began to walk toward the barn, not wanting to get there before Uncle Ernie.

C. T. watched as Uncle Ernie cut through the commotion that was still going on in preparation for the big party. He could only hope that there would actually be a party at the end of this—and not a total disaster.

Both C. T. and Lea kept looking around for any sign of Gus-Gus. Luckily, there was none. C. T. had noticed when they'd passed the henhouse that the door was still shut. Maybe everything would be all right. Maybe Uncle Ernie would get Gus-Gus under control.

"If we ever get out of Bumbleweed alive, I'm never coming back here again," Lea said as they walked along.

"Tell me about it," C. T. agreed. He'd never wanted to come in the first place.

They walked the rest of the way in silence, stopping a good distance from the barn door. Neither of them wanted to look inside.

They didn't have to wait long before Uncle Ernie came racing toward them, carrying a whole jar of pig's feet.

"Mission accomplished," he told them proudly. "Luleen was thrilled that I wanted some of her vittles. As if I would actually eat anything that woman cooked."

"Just get the pill, Uncle Ernie," C. T. urged. This was no time for family gossip.

"I'll be right out," he told them, opening the jar of pig's feet and setting it down on the ground.

Then he rushed into the barn. This time Porkchop didn't follow him. He stood pawing the ground, grunting and oinking.

"I think he's more afraid of Gus-Gus than we are,"

C. T. said to Lea as he nodded toward the pig.

"He's probably seen Gus-Gus in action before," Lea said.

That was not a comforting thought.

"It's going to be all right," C. T. said, more to himself than to Lea—or Porkchop.

"All right," Uncle Ernie said as he stepped out the barn door carrying a pill the size of a golf ball. He reached into the jar, pulled out a foot, and stuffed the huge pill into it. "Let's go get him."

The three of them ran to the henhouse.

"You wait out here," Uncle Ernie told them. He threw open the door to the henhouse, ready to toss in the pig's foot as if it were a live grenade.

His arm went through the motion, but his hand never let go.

"What's wrong?" C. T. asked as Uncle Ernie turned away from the door.

"He's gone," Uncle Ernie informed them. And from the look on Uncle Ernie's face, that was very bad news.

"Where do you think he went?" Lea asked.

"My best guess is the cow pastures," Uncle Ernie said sadly. "We'd better get over there quick before he wipes out the whole herd."

The cow pastures were a good distance from the henhouse. By the time they got there, C. T. had a stitch in his side and was gasping for breath.

Lea and Porkchop were far behind, struggling to keep pace.

But Uncle Ernie was pumped up with adrenaline, thanks to lightning bolt number nine. In fact, he was moving *faster* than lightning. He was already counting heads of cattle before C. T. got to the fence.

"All present and accounted for," Uncle Ernie announced as Lea and Porkchop reached the fence. "Gus-Gus has not been here yet."

"Is that good news?" Lea asked, gasping for air.

"It's good news for the cows," Uncle Ernie answered. "But it's bad news for us, because it means Gus-Gus is looking for his next meal somewhere else."

"Like where?" C. T. asked. He was terrified that Gus-Gus was in the farmhouse eating people while Uncle Ernie was busy counting cows.

"I just hope he hasn't gone into town," Uncle Ernie said before he took off running again.

C. T. couldn't believe a man Uncle Ernie's age could move that fast. He had to struggle to keep up. Lea and Porkchop didn't have a chance. They fell farther and farther behind as Uncle Ernie headed back toward the house.

As C. T. forced his aching legs to keep moving, he wondered how long it had been since he and Lea had first seen Gus-Gus in the henhouse. He figured that at least an hour had passed since then. That was a lot of time. As fast as Gus-Gus could move, he could have gone anywhere and eaten anything—or anybody.

"What are we going to do now?" C. T. asked Uncle Ernie when he caught up with him.

"We're going to make sure that everything is all right at the house, and then we're going to get into the Jeep and head into town," Uncle Ernie answered. "If Gus-Gus isn't there, at least we'll be able to get your grandpa and Uncle Earl to help us look for him."

As they began to close in on the house, C. T. saw something strange.

Uncle Ernie must have seen it too, because he picked up his pace at the same time C. T. did.

There was a huge cloud of dust moving up the dirt path that led from the main road to the house. It looked like a tornado.

That was all that they needed, C. T. thought—a natural disaster to add to the *un*natural one they already had on their hands.

But the dust cloud that was moving up the path wasn't a tornado at all. It was something much, much worse.

CHAPTER 23

Gus-Gus was rolling toward the house in a fury.

Everyone who was out on the lawn still setting up for the party stopped to look at him.

"Run! Run!" C. T. shouted to them.

But no one paid attention to him. They just stared at the curious sight.

Gus-Gus was even bigger now than the last time C. T. had seen him. Rolled up into a tight ball, Gus-Gus was about five feet tall. C. T. couldn't imagine how big he would be if he straightened up and stood on his hind legs. And he didn't want to find out.

Lea screamed as a terrible roar rocked the ground.

But it wasn't coming from Gus-Gus. It was coming from behind him.

Something was following Gus-Gus. C. T. couldn't see

what it was through the dense cloud of dust that the monster kicked up.

"What the heck is that?" C. T. hollered at Uncle Ernie as the steady roar continued.

Uncle Ernie stopped running and stared for a moment. But before he could answer, C. T. saw for himself.

Uncle Earl's pickup truck was following Gus-Gus, getting closer and closer to the monster every second.

"What's he doing?" C. T. asked Uncle Ernie.

Again, Uncle Ernie didn't have to answer.

The truck smashed into Gus-Gus with a horrifying *splat* and rolled right over him. Then it came to a screeching halt.

C. T. heard the gears of the truck grind and watched it speed backward.

There was a loud *thud,* then the screech of brakes once again.

C. T. struggled to see what had happened. But he caught only a glimpse before the truck jolted forward again.

"Earl, you fool," Uncle Ernie shouted, running toward the truck.

Lea came up beside C. T., who hadn't moved. "What's going on?" she cried.

"Uncle Earl smashed Gus-Gus with his truck," C. T. answered.

"Do you think he killed him?" Lea asked.

"I sure hope so," C. T. answered.

But his hopes were short-lived.

Even as Uncle Earl was putting the truck into reverse again, Gus-Gus rose up on his hind legs, towering over the truck, and let out a terrible growl.

The noise that came from the monster drowned out the sound of the truck as it sped backward.

This time when the truck hit Gus-Gus, it didn't roll over him. It stopped.

C. T. watched in shock as Gus-Gus lifted the back end of the truck off the ground and held it there as the wheels spun furiously.

Both doors of the truck flew open and Grandpa and Uncle Earl leaped out. As they scrambled to get away from the truck, Gus-Gus lifted it effortlessly and tossed it onto the lawn.

Pandemonium broke out. People ran in all directions, screaming hysterically.

Gus-Gus just stood there, looking down on them as if he were trying to decide who to go after first.

Meanwhile, Uncle Earl and Uncle Ernie had gotten into a fistfight, which Grandpa was trying to break up.

"Why did you have to go and run over him?" Uncle Ernie shouted at Uncle Earl. "You knew it wouldn't do any good. All you've done is made him mad."

"You idiot," Uncle Earl hollered back. "How did you let him get loose? He was in town. You're lucky we saw him and chased him home before he caused any real trouble."

C. T. didn't think it was so lucky that Gus-Gus was home. Nor did the rest of the family, who were all screaming their heads off.

Gus-Gus growled again. For a moment, everyone was shocked into silence.

Uncle Ernie broke free from Uncle Earl and Grandpa and rushed toward the monster. He still had Aunt Luleen's pig's foot in his hand. He waved it in the air.

"Look what I've got for you," he said. He tossed the pig's foot toward Gus-Gus.

Gus-Gus opened his mouth wide and caught it. He snapped his huge jaws shut and swallowed.

C. T. held his breath, hoping that the tranquilizer would kick in fast. He waited for Gus-Gus to fall over, sound asleep, just like the animals on the TV wildlife shows did after they'd been tranquilized.

But that didn't happen.

Instead of becoming sleepy, Gus-Gus became more ferocious. It was as if that little morsel of food whetted his appetite. He wanted more. He let out another fearsome growl and began flailing his giant claws. His horrific black eyes fixed on Uncle Earl.

And then he moved forward.

C. T. was sure that Uncle Ernie's belief that Gus-Gus would not eat family members was about to be shattered. In fact, C. T. was sure that if somebody didn't do something to stop him, Gus-Gus was going to eat them all!

CHAPTER

24

"I've got an idea," C. T. said to Lea.

"What is it?" she asked hopefully.

"There's no time to explain," he said. "Just follow me."

The two of them took off running again.

"Where are we going?" Lea asked.

"To the old barn," C. T. answered. He didn't tell her any more than that. He was busy thinking of a plan to destroy Gus-Gus.

Uncle Ernie had said it was impossible to kill Gus-Gus. But C. T. was pretty sure that nobody had ever tried what he had in mind. It had to work—or they were all goners.

C. T. and Lea made it to the old barn in record time.

"Grab the jar of Aunt Luleen's pig's feet," C. T. instructed Lea.

"What for?" she asked, sounding defeated. "What are

you going to do, feed him more tranquilizers? I don't think that will work."

"Neither do I," C. T. said. "We're going to feed him something much more powerful than tranquilizers. But we've got to hurry."

C. T. gestured for Lea to follow him. Then he dashed toward the new barn, where Grandpa and Uncle Earl had been arguing the day before. He just hoped that all of Uncle Earl's stuff was still there.

He held his breath as he rounded the corner, then let out a huge sigh of relief when he saw that the tarp was still bulging with the pile of goodies that lay beneath it.

Quickly, C. T. threw back the tarp and dove for the thing he needed to effect his plan—Uncle Earl's box of TNT.

"What are you going to do with that?" Lea shrieked. "That's dynamite! That stuff is really, really dangerous!"

"Let's hope so," C. T. said, digging into the box.

"You'll blow us all to kingdom come," Lea hollered.

"Not all of us," C. T. assured her. "Just Gus-Gus." He pulled out a half dozen sticks of dynamite. "Give me those pig's feet," he said to Lea.

Reluctantly, she handed them over. "I really don't think this is such a good idea," she protested.

"Have you got a better one?" C. T. asked as he reached into the jar and pulled out a foot.

She didn't answer.

"Then this is the only plan we've got to save the family." He stuffed the first stick of dynamite into the foot. "Help me out here," he said to Lea, going for a second.

In no time at all, they had a half dozen pig's feet stuffed with sticks of dynamite. C. T. scooped them off the ground. "Now all we've got to do is feed them to Gus-Gus," he told Lea. "Come on."

The two of them raced back toward the house.

"Feeding the dynamite to Gus-Gus won't be a problem," Lea said between gulps of air as she struggled to keep going. "He'll eat anything. But how are you going to ignite the dynamite?"

"Don't worry about it," C. T. said. "I know exactly what I'm going to do. Trust me." He only wished that he was as sure of himself as he sounded.

Back at the house, Gus-Gus was holding the whole family hostage. Everyone was huddled together on the porch except for Uncle Ernie, who was keeping Gus-Gus at bay by feeding him all the food that had been prepared for Grandpa's birthday party.

C. T. and Lea got there just in time. There wasn't much food left.

"Run into the house and get me the bag of marshmallows," C. T. told Lea.

She hesitated for a moment, looking at C. T. as if he were completely crazy.

"Go!" C. T. demanded.

As she made her way toward the house, C. T. ran toward Uncle Ernie.

"Hey, Gus-Gus," C. T. called. "Have some more of Aunt

Luleen's pig's feet." He tossed one at the monster.

Gus-Gus snapped it up hungrily.

C. T. tossed another.

Gus-Gus went for that one too.

So far, so good, C. T. thought. His plan was working.

Gus-Gus ate up all six pig's feet in no time flat.

"We're almost out of food," Uncle Ernie said nervously. "The tranquilizer still hasn't kicked in. I've never seen Gus-Gus so out of control. There's no telling what he'll do next."

"Lea!" C. T. hollered, looking for her in the crowd on the porch.

It seemed like forever before she shoved her way through, carrying the bag of marshmallows. Her parents tried to hold her back, but she broke free and ran toward C. T.

"I hope you know what you're doing," she said as she handed over the bag.

"Just get back on the porch with everybody else," he told her. "And hope this works."

"What are you up to?" Uncle Ernie asked C. T. as he tossed the last bits of food to Gus-Gus.

"You'll see," C. T. said. He tore open the bag and ran toward the barbecue.

Luckily, it was already ablaze, heating up for Grandma's famous ribs—which Gus-Gus had already eaten raw. But that fire wasn't going to go to waste. It was exactly what C. T. needed.

He snatched a stick off the ground and shoved a

handful of marshmallows onto it. Then he touched them to the fire and dashed back toward Gus-Gus.

"Eat this, you giant fur ball!" he screamed, pitching the stick with the flaming marshmallows toward Gus-Gus.

Gus-Gus was in such a feeding frenzy that he snapped it up the same way he'd gobbled everything else they'd thrown to him.

For a moment, nothing happened.

C. T. was terrified that his plan had failed.

Then Gus-Gus opened his mouth and let out a huge, flaming belch, like a fire-breathing dragon.

The flame singed the grass as it sent Gus-Gus shooting up into the air.

C. T. watched in stunned amazement as Gus-Gus was propelled higher. And higher. And higher. Until . . .

The monster exploded high above their heads like fireworks on the Fourth of July.

CHAPTER 25

C. T. was a hero. He'd saved the whole family from disaster and made Grandpa's birthday a real celebration, even though there was no food left for the feast.

Only Uncle Ernie was a little sad about losing Gus-Gus. After all, Uncle Ernie had spent most of his life taking care of Gus-Gus. And most of the time, Gus-Gus hadn't been a big, scary monster, but a cute, little fur ball. But in the end, even Uncle Ernie had to admit that getting rid of him was all for the best.

Fortunately, Gus-Gus *hadn't* eaten one of the Bobs' Twins. Gus-Gus had only gotten her bow. April—or maybe it was May—had managed to escape unharmed. C. T. still couldn't tell the difference between the two of them.

On the morning after Grandpa's birthday, everybody

packed up to leave. The family reunion was finally over. And despite the happy ending, C. T. couldn't get out of Bumbleweed fast enough.

C. T. and Lea stood on the porch as the rest of the family exchanged tearful good-byes with promises to "do it again real soon." C. T. hoped those promises were just polite lies. If he never did this again in his life, he would be perfectly content. He hoped that from now on Grandma and Grandpa would come to their houses to visit the way they always had before.

After all the hugging and kissing was finished, everyone climbed into their cars, trucks, and Jeeps to leave.

Grandma and Grandpa and Uncle Ernie stood on the porch waving good-bye.

The caravan of vehicles carrying Uncle Earl's clan moved out first. Then C. T.'s dad followed, driving his minivan.

He and Lea's dad were in the front seats. The moms were in the middle seats, and C. T. and Lea were in the back.

"That was some weekend," C. T.'s dad sighed as he honked the horn in one final farewell.

"It certainly was," C. T.'s mom agreed. "I always knew your family was a little strange," she said to her husband. "But who knew they included a monster?"

Everyone laughed nervously.

"Please," C. T.'s dad said. "Let's just try to forget about the whole thing."

"Good idea," Lea's dad agreed.

Lea's mom turned around in her seat to face C. T. and Lea. "I hope you two won't be telling stories to all your friends when we get home," she said.

"Don't worry about it," C. T. assured her. "Nobody would believe us anyway."

"I wouldn't have believed it myself if I hadn't seen it with my own two eyes," Lea's mom said.

"I'm just glad it over," Lea said as she sunk down in her seat.

They rode along in silence for a long, long time.

C. T. had begun to doze off when his father's voice startled him.

"What the heck is that?" C. T.'s father shouted as the minivan swerved hard to the right.

"I don't know," Lea's father said. "But it sure is strange."

Instinctively, everyone looked out their windows to see what was out there.

"It looks like tumbleweeds," C. T.'s mom said.

"I don't know," Lea's mom said nervously. "They're moving awfully fast for tumbleweeds. And there are so many of them!"

C. T. stared out the window at the "tumbleweeds" for a moment. Then he turned to look at Lea, who was already facing him, her eyes wide with terror. She was thinking the same thing C. T. was thinking.

They hadn't killed Gus-Gus at all. They'd only blown him into a thousand little bits—a thousand little monsters.

"Those aren't tumbleweeds," C. T. said, the words barely making it past the knot in his throat.

"Then what on earth are they?" C. T.'s father asked.

C. T. didn't have time to answer.

The little creatures answered for themselves.

All at once, they stopped rolling and stood up. A thousand little monsters surrounded the minivan, each one a clone of Gus-Gus.

"Drive!" C. T.'s mother shrieked.

But C. T.'s father had already floored it, zooming past the monsters as fast as the minivan would go.

C. T. and Lea turned to look out the back window, hoping to see the monsters disappear from sight.

But that wasn't what they saw.

The little monsters were following them, rolling along with great speed.

"Faster, Dad," C. T. cried. "Go faster. They're gaining on us."

The gears on the minivan whined as C. T.'s dad kicked it into overdrive. "It's going to be all right," he assured the rest of them. "We're going to lose those little suckers."

C. T. could only hope he was right—especially since nobody had packed any pig's feet.

Are you ready for more . . .

*Here's a preview of the next spine-chilling book
from A. G. Cascone*

NIGHTMARE ON PLANET X

*The last thing Nicky remembers is being on a plane with
his family, headed for his grandma's house. He knows that
something has gone terribly wrong. He knows they never
made it to Grandma's. What he doesn't know yet is just
how far away from home he really is.*

When Nicky Gogol finally opened his eyes, he had no
idea where he was. He was groggy and weak—and
totally disoriented. Every inch of his body felt heavy. His
head was throbbing so badly, he was afraid his brain was
going to burst right through his eyeballs.

Mom?

Nicky tried to call out to his mother. But his tongue felt
swollen and dry, as though it was wrapped up in cotton.
Nicky could barely swallow, much less speak.

Where am I?

Nicky tried to lift his head. That was a big mistake. Dangling directly above Nicky's face was a blinding white light that seemed to be coming from the center of a huge metal hat. The beam of the light was so hot and bright that Nicky thought it would burn holes through his eyes.

Nicky jerked his head back.

That was a bigger mistake.

Nicky's skull crashed down onto a cold, metal slab beneath him, sending a surge of pain straight to his brain.

Ooooooooo-uch! Nicky's scream echoed through his head as an eerie sound echoed through the room.

It sounded like some kind of sonar blip or radar bleep, but it was high-pitched and haunting.

Be-beep, be-beep, be-beep.

The sound bounced off the cold, sterile walls, piercing Nicky's eardrums like daggers.

Nicky tried to cover his ears—but he couldn't lift his arms.

He tried to sit up—but his waist wouldn't bend, and his legs wouldn't budge.

What the heck is going on?

Below him, Nicky could see dozens of wires snaked across the granitelike floor. Each one led to the monitor of a giant computer. But it wasn't a normal computer. It was a big black box that hung from a long silver pole.

The front of it was covered with knobs and flashing green lights. Above the knobs, the snakelike wires were plugged into tiny round sockets.

The whole box was shaking and beeping like crazy . . .

Until Nicky glanced down at his chest.

Suddenly, the beeping came to a stop.

The wires weren't just plugged into the computer. They were attached to Nicky's chest with dozens of round, little rubbery things that seemed to be sucking his skin off!

"Somebody help me!" Nicky's voice finally burst through his dry, cracked lips.

Panic immediately set in, jump-starting Nicky's heart.

The machine beeped wildly again.

Nicky tried to sit up—but his body was pinned to the metal slab he was lying on. Huge leather straps tied around his arms and his legs held him in place. They were strapped so tightly, they were starting to cut off his circulation.

Nicky could hardly catch his breath.

The air in the room was unlike any air Nicky had ever breathed before. It was thick and musty. Nicky could actually see strange little particles flying through it. He began to panic, fearing the particles would fly up his nose and begin to gnaw at his lungs.

Calm down! Nicky ordered himself, taking one slow breath after the next. *It's silly to panic.* At least that's what Nicky's dad always said when *he* was in scary situations. *There has to be a logical explanation for this.*

But what?

Nicky racked his brain trying to remember where he was and how he had gotten there. But his head was still in a fog. It took him forever just to remember what day it was—or at least what day he *thought* it was.

It's Friday, Nicky told himself. *Mom and Dad and Zoe and I were flying out to see Grandma . . .*

Just then, terror tore through Nicky's heart like a laser as he began to remember the horrible thing that had happened.

Our plane went down! Nicky recalled. *We crashed! I must be in a hospital!*

But Nicky was only half right.

He wasn't in a hospital.

And the horrors about to unfold had nothing to do with a plane crash.

About the Author

A. G. Cascone is the pseudonym of two authors who happen to be sisters . . . "The Twisted Sisters." In addition to *Deadtime Stories*, they have written six books, two horror-movie screenplays, and several pop songs, including one top-ten hit.

If you want to find out more about DEADTIME STORIES or A. G. Cascone, look on the World Wide Web at: http://www.bookwire.com/titles/deadtime/

Also, we'd love to hear from you! You can write to:
A. G. Cascone
c/o Troll
100 Corporate Drive
Mahwah, NJ 07430

Or you can send e-mail directly to:
agcascone@bookwire.com

Read all of the silly, spooky, cool, and creepy

VISIT PLANET TROLL

A super-sensational spot on the Internet

at http://www.troll.com

Check out Kids' T-Zone, a really cool place where you can...

- ✦ Play games!
- ✷ Win prizes!
- ● Speak your mind in the Voting Voice Box!
- 🪐 Find out about the latest and greatest books and authors!
- ★ Shop at BookWorld!
- 🛸 Order books on-line!

And a UNIVERSE more of GREAT BIG FUN!

To order a free Internet trial with CompuServe's Internet access service, Sprynet, adults may call 1-888-947-2669. (For a limited time only.)